ATTICUS THE STORYTELLER'S
100 GREEK MYTHS

ATTICUS THE STORYTELLER'S 100 GREEK MYTHS

Lucy Coats
Illustrated by Anthony Lewis

TED SMART

First published in Great Britain in 2002 by
ORION CHILDREN'S BOOKS
a division of the Orion Publishing Group Ltd
Orion House
5 Upper St Martin's Lane
London   WC2H 9EA

This edition produced for
The Book People Ltd
Hall Wood Avenue
Haydock
St Helens WA11 9UL

A catalogue record for this book is available from the British Library
Printed in Italy by Printer Trento S.r.l.
ISBN 1 84255 026 8

For June 'Bug' Vallance and Ruth M. Rudge, inspirational headmistresses, impeccable classicists, and memorable teachers.

Thanks are also due to the following: Judith Elliott, Rosemary Sandberg and Wendy Cooling for believing in me. Jane Webb and Stuart Squire for trusting me with their books. Katie Paynter for arranging readings and the WHS pupils for listening and appreciating. Brue Richardson for keeping me sane. The internet sites www.perseus.csad.ox.ac.uk and www.pantheon.org/mythica for providing useful maps and information. Anthony Lewis and Kathryn Caulfield-Lewis, and Fiona Kennedy for inspired art, design and editing. And last, but never least, Mum, Richard, Archie and Tabitha for hugs, love, support and patience.

L.C.

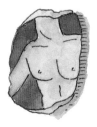

For Paul.

And with thanks to my wife, Kathryn for all of her help with this book.

A.L.

Contents

CONTENTS

CONTENTS

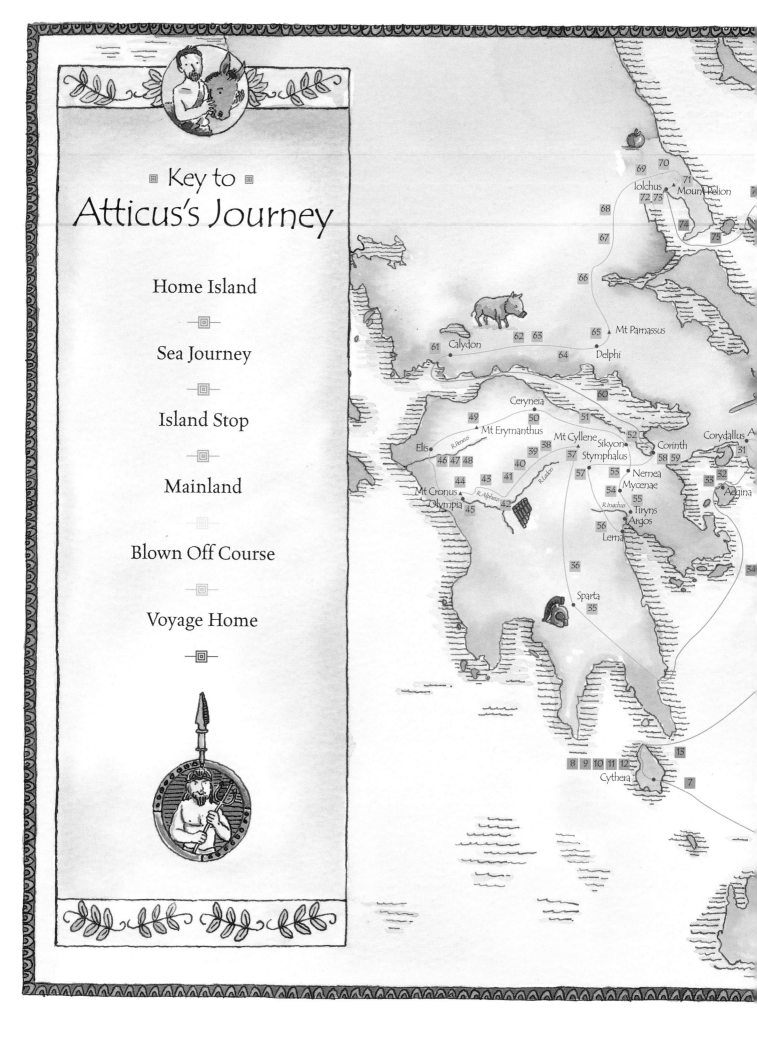

Key to
Atticus's Journey

Home Island

—◻—

Sea Journey

—◻—

Island Stop

—◻—

Mainland

—◻—

Blown Off Course

—◻—

Voyage Home

—◻—

69 70

Iolchus 71
72 73 ▲ Mount Pelion

68

67 74

75

66

62 63 65 ▲ Mt Parnassus

61 Calydon 64 Delphi

60

Ceryneia 51

49 50

▲ Mt Erymanthus 52 Corydallus

R.Peneus Mt Cyllene Sikyon Corinth 31

Elis 39 38 37 Stymphalus 58 59

46 47 48 40 57 53 Nemea 32

44 43 41 R.Ladon 54 Mycenae Aegina

Mt Cronus R.Alpheus 42 55 Tiryns

Olympia 45 R.Inachus Argos

56 Lerna

36 34

Sparta

35

13

8 9 10 11 12 7

Cythera

Lemnos

81

77

78

80

79 · Euboea

29

28

26

27

Chios

25

Mount Sipylus

24

23

· Colophon

22

Mount Latmus

18

Delos

19

15 16

17

Seriphos

14

20 21

Naxos

Troy

82
83

84 85 86 87 88

89

Mount Ida

90 91 92 93 94 95
96 97 98 99 100

6

5

4

· Miletus

1

2

3

Mount Ida

Ionia
ticus
s Here

Stories From the Heavens

Long ago, in Ancient Greece, gods and goddesses, heroes and heroines lived together with fearful monsters and every kind of fabulous beast that ever flew, or walked or swam. But little by little, as people began to build more villages and towns and cities, the gods and monsters disappeared into the secret places of the world and the heavens, so that they could have some peace. And although there were still heroes and heroines around (and always will be), they were less famous and less strong with every century that passed.

Before they disappeared, the gods and goddesses gave the gift of storytelling to men and women, so that nobody would ever forget them. They ordered that there should be a great storytelling festival once every seven years on the slopes of Mount Ida, near Troy, and that tellers of tales should come from all over Greece and from lands near and far to take part. Every seven years a beautiful painted vase, filled to the brim with gold, magically appeared as a first prize, and the winner was honoured for the rest of his life by all the people of Greece.

Atticus the Storyteller Sets Out

Now a little after those long ago times there was a sandalmaker called Atticus who lived in a little village to the east of the great city of Cydonia in Crete, with his wife Trivia, his nine children (eight girls and a boy), Melissa his donkey, Circe his pig, Scylla his cow, Phaëthon his cockerel, and twenty-four speckled hens (who had no names because the fox was always eating them).

Atticus was a very good sandalmaker, but he was an even better storyteller. The children of the village were always popping into the shop to ask for a quick story, and Atticus was always happy to oblige, because he claimed that the stories got into his sandals and made the feet in them walk along faster.

What Atticus really wanted was to tell his stories in the competition at the great storytelling festival of the gods at Troy. He had never quite managed it, because on the way there he wanted to visit the places where the gods were born, and see where all the monsters lived. Then he wanted to sail to Troy just like the kings and princes had done in the great war. The journey would take months, so what with the children's coughs and Scylla having a calf and Trivia having a new baby he'd never been able to spare the time before. It was now or never.

So Atticus decided that he would leave his only son, Geryon, in charge of the sandal shop, the girls in charge of the animals, and Trivia in charge of everyone.

One fine morning in late autumn Atticus packed his bags and loaded Melissa the donkey.

He wiped his eyes and blew his nose noisily before he hugged his wife and children seven times for luck and set off, shouting goodbyes and last-minute instructions as he went.

Nine grubby handkerchiefs and one clean one waved and waved in the distance as Atticus the Storyteller and Melissa the donkey walked down the track away from the bay of Cydonia and towards the port of Miletus.

"I hope Geryon keeps my tools sharp," he muttered. "And I wonder whether the girls will remember to shut the hens up at night. Perhaps I should just . . . Melissa snorted and marched on firmly, her small hooves throwing up puffs of white dust.

"Oh well, I suppose you're right," sighed Atticus. "We must start, or we shall never get there. Shall we have a story to set us on our way?" He looked at Mount Ida far to the south. "Let's begin at the very beginning."

▣ 1 ▣

Father Sky and Mother Earth

In the time before time began there was only Gaia, the beautiful Earth, and her husband Uranus, the Sky. Uranus loved Gaia so much that he wrapped his great black cloak of twinkling stars about her, and danced her all around the heavens.

Soon they had twelve beautiful children called the Titans, who became the first gods and goddesses. But then lovely Gaia gave birth to more children, and they were not beautiful at all. Uranus hated the ugly one-eyed Cyclopes babies as soon as he saw them, and when he was shown the hideous hundred-armed monsters that came next, he roared with rage, and locked them all up in the dreadful land of Tartarus, which lay deep in the depths of the Underworld.

Gaia was very angry, because she loved all her children whatever they looked like, and she vowed to punish Uranus. She gave a magic stone sickle to Cronus, her youngest son, and sent him to fight his powerful father. Cronus was dreadfully frightened, but he loved his mother, and always obeyed her. So he hid in a fold of his father's cloak, and waited till Uranus was not looking. Then Cronus gave Uranus such a great wound with the sickle that Uranus fled into the furthest part of the heavens and never returned.

Then Gaia married Pontus the Sea, who covered her body with his beautiful rainbow waters, and as a sign of her love for him, she gave birth to the trees and flowers and beasts and birds, and every kind of creature, including people. And for many many moons there was peace and harmony in every part of the earth.

By evening, Atticus and Melissa had begun to climb the steep slopes of Mount Ida. The village was an invisible dot on the horizon behind them. There was a huge cave above them, with a great stone lying beside it.

"That reminds me of another story about Cronus. Would you like to hear it?" Melissa gave a hee-haw, and tossed her head.

2
The Stone Baby

Cronus now ruled over all that was, and soon he married his sister Rhea, the most beautiful of all the Titans. But he always remembered what he had done to his father Uranus, and he was frightened that one of his own children might do the same to him. So as each child was born, he opened his enormous mouth wide wide wide and swallowed it in one big gulp.

Rhea was very sad that she could never see her children, and she tried to persuade Cronus to let her keep just one. But Cronus just shook his head and patted his big belly.

"They are quite safe in here, my dear," he boomed. "I can feel them all wriggling around!"

Rhea decided to ask Gaia for advice.

"When the next child is born, you must play a trick on Cronus," said Gaia. "You must get an enormous stone, and wrap it up just like a baby. Keep it beside you, and when Cronus asks you for the child, give him the stone instead, and hide the real baby somewhere safe." So that is just what Rhea did.

She took the child (whom she named Zeus) to a cave on Mount Ida. Then she summoned some noisy sprites, and told them to play loud music around the cave mouth, so that Cronus wouldn't hear Zeus when he cried.

Cronus never noticed a thing. The baby gods and goddesses inside him grew and grew, and kicked and kicked to get out. They used the heavy stone which Rhea had made him swallow as a football inside his tummy, and this made Cronus very cross and uncomfortable as he strode about his business across the heavens and around the earth. And the rumbles his stomach made because of it were the first thunder ever heard.

The cool blue light of dawn shone on the eastern slopes of Mount Ida as Atticus and Melissa looked back. Although they had only been walking for a day the sandal shop and the family seemed far away already, and they still had a long way to go before they even reached the harbour at Miletus.

"Let's have another story to keep us cheerful," said Atticus.

◙ 3 ◙
King of the Gods, Lord of the Universe

Rhea sent a magical goat called Amaltheia and some of her favourite nymphs to look after baby Zeus in the cave on Mount Ida. Amaltheia's milk, which tasted of ambrosia and nectar, made him strong and tall in no time at all, and soon he was as powerful as his great father, Cronus.

When Amaltheia died, he gave her horns to the nymphs, to thank them for looking after him so well. They were magic horns of plenty, and whatever food or drink you wished for would pour out of them as soon as you asked for it. Zeus made Amaltheia's skin into magic armour, which nothing could pierce, and strode out into the world.

Rhea sent him a wife, called Metis, who was very wise. Metis told Zeus that he mustn't attack his father until he had some powerful friends to help him, and she knew just how to get them for him by a clever trick.

Zeus hid behind a tree, while Metis dressed up as an old herbwoman, and waited by the side of the road till Cronus went past.

"Try my herbs of power," she croaked. "Never be defeated! Overcome all your enemies!" Cronus was very interested, for lately he had suspected that Rhea was plotting against him.

"I'll take some," he said, and soon he had swallowed down a big bottle of disgusting green liquid. It was extremely bitter and tasted horrid. All of a sudden he began to feel sick. Then he *was* very sick indeed. Zeus and Metis watched as first a great stone, and then all five of Cronus's other children came up one by one out of his wide wide wide mouth. Zeus ran out from behind his tree to join Hades and Poseidon, Hestia, Demeter and Hera, who were all furious with Cronus for trapping them for so long. Cronus took one look at their angry faces and ran away, leaving his powers behind him on the road. Zeus picked them up and put them in his pocket.

"Now I'm Lord of the Universe," he boomed. And all the world heard him, and shivered at his powerful voice.

Several long days later Atticus and Melissa reached the harbour at Miletus. It was bustling with people as they pushed their way through the market of fishsellers and clothmakers and potters. The boat which would take them to Cythera was bobbing up and down at the quayside as passengers and bags and hens and ducks and donkeys got off. There was a queue waiting to get on.

Atticus sat on a bollard and stroked Melissa's ears. "I'll tell you a story while we're waiting," he said.

▣ 4 ▣

The Three Gifts

Now that Zeus had picked up his father Cronus's powers, he was the king of heaven and earth and everywhere in between. But even Zeus was not strong enough to look after the universe all by himself. He called his brothers to a meeting.

"I can't rule the universe properly unless you help me," he said, taking off his helmet. "Why don't we share it out between us?" Hades and Poseidon agreed, and so into the helmet Zeus put a sapphire for the earth and sky, a turquoise for the sea, and a ruby for the Underworld. Since Zeus was

the most powerful, he closed his eyes and picked first. Out came the sapphire. Poseidon picked the turquoise and Hades the ruby. That was how the division of the universe was decided.

But the Titans, who were Zeus's uncles and aunts, did not like this at all. They thought that *they* should have a share in ruling things, so they raised an army to fight Zeus and his brothers.

Zeus immediately freed the Cyclopes and the hundred-armed monsters that his grandfather had imprisoned in Tartarus, to help him. The Cyclopes were so grateful that they made presents for the brothers.

For Poseidon they made a trident which could cause earthquakes and tidal waves.

For Hades they made a helmet of darkness, so that he could sneak up on his enemies without being seen.

And for Zeus they made thunder and lightning bolts which made him so powerful that no one could stand against him.

The Titans were soon beaten, and Zeus banished nearly all of them to Tartarus, where he set the hundred-armed monsters to guard them. Prometheus and Epimetheus, the only two Titans who had supported Zeus, were allowed to go free. But Atlas, the strongest of the Titans, was sent to the far ends of the earth, so that he could carry the weight of the heavens on his shoulders forever.

At last they were on board The Maid of Cythera. Melissa brayed goodbye to Crete as Atticus arranged the bags along the deck of the boat.

A little girl nudged her mother. "Look, Mum! There's Atticus the Storyteller who lives next door to Auntie Hecuba!" she whispered. Atticus smiled at her.

"Would you like to hear a story, little one?" he asked.

"Yes, please! A nice scary one!"

Atticus settled down, and pointed into the far west, where the sun was setting. "The scariest monster I know lives over there, under a great big fiery mountain. His name is Typhon, and this is his story."

▣ 5 ▣

The Volcano Monster

When Gaia learnt that Zeus had trapped her Titan children in Tartarus, she shook with rage. And out of her raging body there appeared two great and horrible monsters called Typhon and Echidna.

Echidna had a woman's head and arms, but her body was like an enormous fat snake, covered in warty spots and spines.

Typhon had a hundred heads, each one dripping with venom and slime. When he roared like a hundred lions or trumpeted like a

herd of elephants, great rivers of boiling mud and fiery stones poured out of his mouths.

When the gods saw him, they were so frightened that they turned themselves into animals and ran far away to hide in the woods.

Typhon tore up enormous mountains by the roots and he hurled them at Zeus and his brothers and sisters, hissing like a thousand snakes. But Zeus was brave, and he called to the other gods to come and help him defeat the monster.

Soon a fierce battle raged over the earth, and everything was destroyed. The gods were tired out and nearly beaten. But as Typhon lifted Mount Etna to throw at Zeus's head, Zeus let fly one of his thunderbolts, and knocked the mountain down on Typhon's heads, trapping him forever.

Echidna fled to a cave in southern Greece when she saw how Zeus had destroyed her mate. There she had her many children, all as hideous as herself, and Zeus allowed them to live in peace, so that the future heroes of Greece could fight them when the time was right.

As for Typhon, he lies wriggling and struggling under Mount Etna to this day, spewing smoke and flames out of the top, and raining down boiling stones on the poor people of Sicily.

The little girl blinked sleepily up at Atticus. "Thank you. Can I have another story now?"

The other passengers looked at him hopefully.

"It makes the journey go quicker," said an old lady clutching a basket of hens on her lap. Atticus looked back towards Crete, a distant black shape in the moonlight. He thought of his family, and of his son Geryon, and how he missed them all already. There was a tower silhouetted against the horizon—a tall tower with a pointed roof.

"I shall tell you a tale of Crete," he said. "A tale of a father and son, and of how one of them reached the stars."

◉ 6 ◉

The Boy Who Fell Out of the Sky

King Minos of Crete was furious. He was seething. He was bubbling with rage. "Bring me Daedalus!" he cried. Daedalus was the king's inventor, and he had designed an impossible maze to keep the king's Minotaur—a horrible bull monster—safe. Now the monster was dead, the king's only daughter had fled, and Minos wanted someone to blame.

So Daedalus was dragged before King Minos' feet in chains, and after the king had kicked him and jumped on him, he was taken to the highest room in the highest tower in the palace at Knossos, and locked in with his son, Icarus, who was ten. They had no food, and no water, and soon they were desperately hungry and thirsty. But Daedalus was very clever, and soon he had a plan of escape.

He made Icarus climb up into the roof, where there was a big old deserted bees' nest. Icarus took all the honeycombs and threw them down to his father. Then he stole the tailfeathers from all the pigeons who were sleeping in the rafters, and threw them down too.

When they had licked some dew off the windowsills and sucked out some honey from the combs, Daedalus melted the beeswax by shining a ray of sun through a magnifying-glass he had in his pocket, and made four big wing shapes out of it. Then, while it was still soft, he pressed the pigeons' feathers into it. He made leather straps from his belt and sandals, and then they were ready.

Daedalus and Icarus strapped their wings onto their shoulders, climbed onto the windowsill, and leapt out into the air. It was quite dark, apart from a few blazing stars, so no one could see them from the ground.

"Wheeee!" shouted Icarus, as he swept through the sky. "I can fly! Look, Dad! I can fly!"

"Keep going west," yelled Daedalus, flapping alongside. "And remember not to fly too high. If the sun catches you when he gets up, he will melt your wings, and you'll fall!"

Icarus was having such a good time he didn't listen. He swooped up to the stars, and pulled Sirius's tail. Then he swooshed round the Great Bear. He didn't notice Helios the sun god driving his great chariot up over the eastern horizon behind him. Helios cracked his whip, and fiery rays of sunshine darted across the sky. One of them touched Icarus's wings, and the beeswax ran like rain down into the ocean far below. A feather brushed Icarus's cheek as he tumbled helplessly to the sea beneath, crying out for his father to save him.

Poor Daedalus could only watch and weep for his lost son as he flew on towards Sicily. As his tears fell into the ocean, they were caught by the nereids and made into pearls of wisdom. And the grandmothers, who know, say that Icarus's spirit rises up from the sea every night, and flies up to the heavens to play with the stars.

Dawn was rising over the island of Cythera as they sailed towards it, and all over the boat people were stretching and yawning as they woke up. Atticus felt a tug on his sleeve.

"Oh, all right, one last story!" he said, smiling at the little girl. "I'll tell you how fire came down to earth, and then I must see to my donkey before we get off."

▣ 7 ▣

How Fire Came to Earth

Zeus wanted to reward Prometheus and Epimetheus, the two Titans who had helped him in battle. So he gave them the job of making new creatures to scamper over the earth, and fill her woods and meadows with songs and joyful sounds once more.

"Here are the things you will need," he said, pointing to a row of barrels. "There's plenty for both of you." And he flew off back to Olympus.

Prometheus set about making some figures out of the first barrel, which was full of clay. He shaped two kinds of bodies, and rolled out long sausages of mud and pressed them against the bodies to make arms and legs. Then he made two round balls, and stuck them on the tops. He hummed as he worked, and his clever fingers shaped ears and eyes and hair and mouths until the figures looked just like tiny copies of Zeus and his wife. It took him a very long time, because he wanted his creations to be perfect.

In the time that Prometheus had made his two sorts of figures, Epimetheus had made many. First he used up the barrels of spots, then he used all the stripes; he simply flung handfuls of bright feathers about, and as for the whiskers and claws he gave them out twenty at a time! By the time Prometheus had finished his men and women there was not a thing left to give them other than some thin skin, and a little fine hair.

Prometheus went straight to Zeus.

"My creatures are cold!" he said. "You must give me some of your special fire to warm them up, or they will die!" But Zeus refused.

"Fire is only for gods. They will just have to manage," he said. "You shouldn't have been so slow in making them."

Now this annoyed Prometheus a lot. He had taken such care, and his creations had things inside that Epimetheus could never even have *thought* of. So he decided to steal Zeus's fire for them. He sneaked up to Olympus, carrying a hollow reed, and stole a glowing coal from Zeus's hearth. Then he flew down to earth.

"Keep this sacred fire of the gods burning always," he commanded his creatures. And they did. They looked deep into the flames and saw just what they should do. They built temples, and in each temple was a fire. And on the fires they placed offerings to the gods, and the smoke of them reached right up to Zeus's palace on Olympus.

Zeus liked the delicious smell. But when he looked down to earth and saw the fires burning everywhere like little red stars, he was not happy at all.

"Prometheus!" he bellowed. "I told you not to take that fire! I'll make you regret your stealing ways!" He swooped down on the back of a giant eagle and carried Prometheus away to the Caucasus Mountains, where he chained him to the highest peak. And Zeus sent the giant eagle to visit him every morning and tear enormous chunks out of his liver. Every night the liver magically regrew, so that poor Prometheus's punishment was never-ending.

But Zeus never took back the gift of fire from the earth, and we have it still to warm us on cold winter nights.

Atticus and Melissa left the boat behind and trudged along the broad track that led across Cythera. Other donkeys passed them on their way to the busy harbour behind them.

"Did you ever hear the story of Pandora's jar?" asked Atticus, looking at the heavy jars and sacks of grain which the donkeys were carrying. Melissa pricked up her ears. "No? Then I'll tell it to you."

▣ 8 ▣
The Inquisitive Wife

Pandora was the most inquisitive woman on earth. Zeus had made her that way on purpose. She was always asking questions and prying into other people's business.

"Who's this? What's that? Why? Why? Why?" she would ask her poor husband Epimetheus at least a hundred times a day. Epimetheus was very patient, and because Pandora was so pretty and he loved her, he put up with her questions. But one day, as she was poking about, Pandora found a great big jar right in the furthest corner of the attic. It was very heavy, and when she tried to lift it, she couldn't. She ran down to Epimetheus, who was talking to some of the animals he had made.

"Husband! Husband!" she squealed as she saw him. "I've found a lovely big jar, and I want to know what's in it! Come and help me!"

Epimetheus went white as a sheet and began to shake.

"Wife! Wife! You must never never touch that jar! My brother Prometheus gave it to me, and he made me promise that it must never be moved or opened till the end of the world! Promise me that whatever else you do, you will never touch that jar again!" So Pandora promised, and although it was very difficult for her, she kept her promise for at least an hour. But then, oh dear, her curiosity began to get the better of her.

"Surely if I just have a little tiny peek, it won't do any harm!" she said. And she sneaked up to the attic again.

Pandora quickly took the lid off the jar, and poked her nose right in. What a horrible surprise she got when a whole lot of nasty looking insects flew out and started pricking her with their stings. She slammed the lid back on at once, shutting inside the only creature that was left.

"Oh! Oh! Oh!" she shrieked as she ran down the stairs past Epimetheus and out into the garden. "Come and get back in the jar, you horrid little things!" But the insects just buzzed and hummed with shrill little voices and flew off.

Ever since the day Pandora opened that jar, envy and greed, and jealousy and anger and all the other evil things that were shut in there by clever Prometheus have flown about the world, stinging human beings and pricking them all over with their sharp little pins. Only hope was left in the jar—trapped by Pandora right at the very bottom. And as long as hope is there, nothing in the world can ever be quite as bad as it seems.

As darkness fell, Atticus knocked on a cottage door by the roadside. "I wondered if we could stop here for the night?" he asked as the door opened, and several children poured out round his feet. "I could pay with a story."

While Atticus finished his last mouthful of bread and cheese eight pairs of eyes watched him expectantly. He cleared his throat. "A good meal deserves a good tale!" he said. "I'll tell you the story of a great flood."

9

The Greatest Flood

Prometheus had a son called Deucalion, who was good and kind. He loved all the birds and beasts and insects—he even loved the eagle who tore at his father's liver each morning.

"He's only doing his job!" he would say to poor Prometheus, on his yearly visit to the Caucasus. And Prometheus would grit his teeth and nod bravely, as Deucalion stroked the eagle's feathers while they talked.

But one year, Prometheus was brought some terrible tidings by the North Wind. He begged the eagle to take a day off to fetch Deucalion to him. And because Deucalion had been kind to him, the eagle went.

"My son," said Prometheus. "You must save yourself and your wife. Zeus is angry with Pandora for opening my jar and letting all the evils into the world. They have infected my clay people, and now they are being so cruel to each other that Zeus is going to get rid of them. He is going to make it rain and rain, till all the earth is covered, and everything in it is drowned. You must make a boat for yourself and Pyrrha and then you will escape."

"But Father, what about all the animals and birds and insects? They aren't like your people—they are innocent. How can I save *them*?" asked Deucalion.

So Prometheus told him how to build a great ark, with enough room for two of each kind of creature. And soon the whole earth was covered in water, and the only things alive upon it were Deucalion and his wife, and the creatures they had gathered into the ark. It was very smelly, and there wasn't much food, but after nine nights and days the waters went down, and the ark came to land on the top of a great mountain.

The animals and birds and insects scampered and flew and crawled off to find new homes, and Deucalion and Pyrrha knelt on the land and praised Zeus for their escape. They lit a fire with some precious embers they had saved in a pot, and as the smoke reached up to Olympus, Zeus looked down and saw them praying.

"These are good people," he thought. "I shall help them." So he gave a message to the North Wind, Boreas, and sent him to blow it into Deucalion's ear.

"Zeus says to throw the mother's bones over your shoulder!" whistled Boreas. Deucalion was very surprised. Surely Zeus didn't mean Pyrrha's bones.

"Zeus means the bones of Mother Earth, silly!" said Pyrrha. And she picked up a big stone and threw it over her shoulder. Immediately, a little girl stood there. She came running up to Pyrrha to be hugged.

Deucalion and Pyrrha walked all over the earth throwing stones over their shoulders, and in each place they walked Deucalion made men and Pyrrha made women. Some were brown and some were pink, and some were yellow and some were black. And because they were made from stone, Pandora's evil stinging insects were not nearly so harmful to them as they had been to the people Prometheus had made of clay so many years before.

Two days later Atticus and Melissa hurried to take shelter under some great rocks as thunder and lightning flashed and roared over the sea.

"This is just like a storm Zeus once found himself in," said Atticus. "I'll tell you about it."

◻ 10 ◻

The Cuckoo's Trick

Zeus was brave, he was strong, he was handsome—in fact he was the greatest of the gods. So why wouldn't beautiful Hera marry him? He brought her magical flowers that bloomed a different colour each day. He brought her crowns made of moonbeams and necklaces made of starlight. But Hera just looked down her long straight perfect nose and laughed.

"Oh Zeus!" she sighed. "Just leave me alone and go and play with your thunderbolts. I'll never marry you until you can sit on my lap without me noticing—and that will be never!" And Zeus stomped back to his palace in a terrible temper that made the earth below shake and tremble.

Then he had an idea. He would do just what Hera had told him. He *would* go and play with his thunderbolts. Zeus stirred up the most tremendous thunderstorm that ever was. Then he changed himself into a cuckoo, and set out for Hera's palace through the storm. Wet, bedraggled and exhausted, he flew through the window of her bedroom, and landed shaking on her bed.

"Poor little cuckoo!" said Hera, stroking his soaking grey feathers. "Let me dry you." In no time at all the cuckoo was dry and comfortable, and nestling into Hera's lap. Then the cuckoo began to change. It grew and grew until—there was Zeus sitting in Hera's lap, laughing.

"Cuckoo!" he said, kissing her. "Will you marry me now?" And Hera had to agree.

Zeus and Hera were given many amazing wedding presents by all the gods and goddesses, in celebration of their marriage. The most wonderful of all was the magical apple tree given to Hera by Mother Earth. Its fruit was as golden as the sun, and it gave everlasting life to anyone who ate it. Hera planted it in her special garden, and set three beautiful nymphs to guard it, together with Argos, the hundred-eyed monster who never slept. In later times Heracles, the bravest hero of all, stole some of the precious apples, but that is quite another story.

When the storm was over Atticus pulled his wet cloak more closely around his shoulders as they walked northwards.

"Winter will soon be here, Melissa," he said. "I smell frost." Melissa flattened her ears and shivered. The flowers on the hillsides of Cythera were all dying now, and fluffy seed puffs blew across the path as they walked towards the sea.

"This time of year reminds me of Demeter, looking for her beautiful daughter all over the earth." And he began the story.

◻ 11 ◻

The Queen of the Underworld

Demeter, goddess of the harvest, had hair the colour of sunset, and lips and cheeks as pink and perfect as a summer morning. Wherever she walked on the earth, trees would burst into fruit, and corn ripen to burning gold; flowers would waft sweet scents towards her, and vegetables swell and pop with green juicy life.

She had a daughter called Kore, the most lovely child ever born, and it was Demeter's delight to play with her all the long sunny days of summer—and where Demeter was it was always summer. But when Kore was about sixteen years old, she was seen picking flowers in the fields and

woods by Hades, the dark god of the Underworld. Hades fell in love with her at once, but he knew that Demeter would never give permission for him to marry her—he would have to kidnap her instead.

So one bright afternoon Hades drove his chariot pulled by six black horses out of a huge crack in the ground, seized Kore in his arms, and carried her off screaming to his kingdom of Tartarus, deep in the Underworld. Only a little shepherd boy and his brother had seen what had happened and they were too scared to say anything.

For a whole year Demeter travelled in search of her daughter, calling and calling. And while she called, tears ran down her face so fast that it became all wrinkled and crinkled, and her lovely hair turned grey and lank with sadness. Nothing grew or bloomed any more, and the earth became a frozen, dark place, where the North Wind blew snow and ice over the fields, and no birds sang. Men, women and children shivered and shook as they huddled round their fires and starved.

In the heavens, only Helios the sun god had seen what Hades had done. He told Zeus, but as usual, Zeus decided not to interfere with his dark brother's doings. However he soon noticed how cold and unhappy the mortals on earth were. There were no nice-smelling sacrifices to the gods,

no prayers, only misery. He saw at once that he would have to do something after all, and so he sent his messenger, Hermes, to comfort Demeter.

"Don't you worry, my dear. I'll get her back for you," said Hermes, who had just talked to the two shepherd boys and found out where Kore was. And down he went to visit Hades, down down down to Tartarus in the deepest part of the earth, where the dead souls of men and heroes wander like mist.

Now it is well known that if you eat any food from the Underworld, you can never return to the earth. Kore knew this, and so although Hades had tempted her with delicious food and drink, she had not touched a single morsel in all the time she had been there. All she had eaten was three seeds from a pomegranate growing in Hades' garden, when she thought nobody was looking.

When Hermes came to demand that Kore be returned to her mother, Hades smiled a nasty smile.

"Little Kore has been very silly!" he smirked. "She thought nobody would see her. But my gardener was hiding behind a tree, and he swears he saw her spit three pomegranate pips into a bush!" Kore burst into tears. Now she would never escape from her dreary prison, where the sun never shone, and the only birdsong was the cawing of ravens.

But Hermes was very crafty.

"If you don't send Kore back to Demeter, everyone on earth will die from cold and starvation, and you will be so busy sorting the dead souls out that you won't have time to even think, let alone enjoy yourself. Why don't you let her spend a month here for every seed she ate, and the rest with her mother up on the earth?"

Hades knew when he was beaten, and he agreed to Hermes' plan. So Kore went back to her mother for nine months of the year, and the earth bloomed once more. But for the three months that we call winter, Kore now changes her name to Persephone, and goes to live with Hades underground. And the cold winds blow, and the snow falls, and Demeter weeps tears of ice because she misses her daughter so much.

They reached the sea and Melissa trotted happily along the sand behind Atticus. The sun was coming up, it was a beautiful crisp day and her coat was dry again.

"This is where Aphrodite was born," said Atticus, sitting down on a rock to rest, and picking up a piece of green seaweed. "It was like this."

◙ 12 ◙

The Foam Goddess

Many years ago, when Uranus fled into the deepest heavens, one drop of blood from the great wound that his son, Cronus, had given him dripped into the sea and changed into foam.

"We must not waste this precious gift," whispered the waves. And they rushed at the magic foam, and swirled it and whirled it into the shape of the most beautiful goddess of all, Aphrodite. A giant scallop shell was brought up from the depths of the ocean on the back of a whale, and six dolphins were harnessed to it. Then Aphrodite stepped into it and settled onto its pink

velvety cushions while she was blown to the shores of the island of Cythera by the West Wind. As she stepped onto the earth for the first time, clouds of sparrows and doves flew twittering and cooing round her head, and three lovely maidens brought her robes made of sea-spray and rainbows.

When Zeus saw her exquisite beauty, he knew that all the gods would fight over her, so he quickly married her off to his son, the lame blacksmith god Hephaestus.

"That will keep her out of trouble," he thought to himself. Aphrodite was not at all happy about this, for Hephaestus was always black and sooty from the dirt of his forge fires.

"Ugh! Get off!" she snarled, as he kissed her on their wedding night. "Look at your dirty fingerprints all over my clean robe!"

She would much rather have married his brother, handsome Ares, or funny Hermes who teased her and made her laugh. But Aphrodite soon came round when she saw the beautiful things that Hephaestus made for her. The most wonderful of all was a magic golden girdle, set with glittering jewels. Whenever Aphrodite wore it, she was so lovely that no one could resist anything she asked, not even if it was Zeus himself.

Although she lived on Olympus, Aphrodite always went back to her birthplace for a month's holiday every year. And when she came back to her palace, the very flowers bowed beneath her feet in amazement at her shining beauty and grace. She had a little son called Eros whom she thought was the most beautiful child in the world. Together they danced across the earth and the heavens shooting gods and mortals alike with their arrows of love, and as they passed, even the cold hearts of the stars were filled with joy.

Atticus was hot and bothered. He and Melissa had nearly missed the boat from Cythera to Seriphos, and now he was sitting squashed up against some bales of cloth with Melissa beside him. The sea was rough and it was raining. A sailor with a wooden leg was steering a wobbly course past the tip of the mainland.

"He reminds me of the blacksmith god Hephaestus," whispered Atticus in Melissa's ear. "And he's certainly dirty enough to be a smith! I'll tell you the story very quietly, so as not to annoy him."

◙ 13 ◙

The Lame Blacksmith

Hephaestus was the son of Zeus and Hera. As a baby, he was rather small and puny, and he didn't like loud noises. So when his father threw thunderbolts, and his mother shouted, he cowered in his cradle and shivered. As a little boy, though, he grew braver, and one day when his parents were arguing, he tried to stop them.

"You hurt my ears!" he said, glaring at Zeus. "Why don't you both just stop shouting—Yack! Bang! Yell! Yack! Bang! Yell!—I'm fed up with listening to you." Now this made Zeus so angry that he picked Hephaestus up by his ears and flung him down to earth.

Hephaestus fell for a whole day, and when he landed feet first on the island of Lemnos, his leg bones shattered into tiny pieces, and he fainted from the pain. There Thetis the sea-nymph found him, and carried him to her cave, where she and her daughter looked after him for nine whole years.

Because Hephaestus was now lame, and couldn't get around easily, he amused himself by making beautiful things with his strong hands, and soon he was the cleverest smith and jeweller that ever lived.

One day Hera met Thetis at a party, and admired her dolphin brooch, made of sea pearls and sapphires.

"Where did you get that?" she asked. "I must have one myself!" When she discovered that it was her own son who was the craftsman, she carried him straight to Olympus and made Zeus apologise and set him up as official blacksmith to the gods. Zeus was very sorry for what he had done, and that was why he chose Hephaestus to be Aphrodite's husband.

Hephaestus built a smithy deep in the heart of the mountains, with twenty bellows worked by the Cyclopes, who became his assistants. Among the amazing things he made were two robots of silver and gold, which would do anything he asked. And when the gods had meetings, they used his little magic tables, which ran around on golden wheels, taking food and drink to anyone who needed it.

It was still raining, and the boat to Seriphos was crowded with goods, people and animals. Atticus kept pushing an inquisitive pig away from him.

"This cloth must be going to Tyre to be dyed," he said to the man with the pig. "I'd love a Tyrrhenian blue cloak, but they're so expensive." The pig's owner grunted.

"Wish this boat would hurry up," he said. "I hate the sea."

"Would you like me to tell you a story to pass the time?" Atticus asked.

The pig man grunted again. "Go on then!" He closed his eyes as Atticus began.

▣ 14 ▣

The Bull From the Sea

Zeus loved his birthplace, Crete. He knew every rocky inch of it, the way the hills smelled of thyme in the sunshine, the way the dark sea sounded when it rushed against the shore. He knew the little white villages, and the narrow ledges where the seagulls nested, and the caves where bats hung from dark crevices in the stone.

"Crete needs a queen," he thought one day, as he flew back to Olympus. "But where can I find a woman good and beautiful enough to take care of my beloved island for me?" Zeus looked and looked whenever he visited earth. But every woman he saw was either too tall or too short, too fat or too thin, too chatty or too silent. Not one woman came close to what he wanted until one day, flying over the city of Tyre, he saw a girl playing on the seashore with some of her friends.

"Ha!" said Zeus, making himself invisible. "This is the one. She's perfect!"

Europa was the King of Tyre's daughter. She had long dark hair as shiny as chestnuts, and grey eyes that turned as blue as dye when she was happy. They were blue now, but they quickly changed back to grey as she looked at the sea and saw a great white bull wading up towards her out of the waves. At first, Europa and her friends were frightened, but when the bull lay down quietly on the shore and looked at them through his long silky eyelashes, they came closer and stroked his furry flanks. The bull snorted softly, and his breath smelled of violets.

"Ooh, isn't he sweet?" squealed Europa. "Do let's make some garlands for his horns, and then we can take him back to the palace and keep him as a pet!" So the girls ran into the meadows by the beach and picked some sea pinks and cistus and wove them into garlands. Europa was the tallest, so she climbed onto the bull's broad back to slip them over his sharp horns. As she knelt astride his shoulders, the bull got up and started to gallop out to sea along a great road of shining water that had suddenly appeared. Europa's friends screamed and ran after him into the waves, but it was no good—the bull had vanished as quickly as he had come.

Europa was a brave girl, so she was not a bit surprised when the bull spoke to her as he ran.

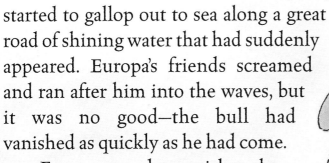

"I am Zeus, greatest of the gods," he bellowed. "I have chosen you to be Queen of Crete. I shall marry you as my mortal wife, and we will have fine sons together."

And what Zeus said came true. After he had married Europa, and given her a crown of beautiful jewels, they had three strong sons. Europa ruled happily in the palace Zeus built for her, and she was helped by a marvellous bronze robot called Talos, which Hephaestus had made for her on Zeus's orders. Talos clanked around the island on his metal legs three times a day, and if an enemy ship came near, he threw rocks at it. Together, Talos and Europa kept Crete safe from any enemies for many long years.

It was a great relief when they landed on the island of Seriphos.

"Pooh!" said Atticus. "That pig was smelly. I need a wash!" Melissa wrinkled her nose and trotted on fast towards a little spring by the roadside. Atticus washed his hands and face and sat down.

"This is where the hero Perseus was brought up," he said. "I'll tell you the story."

◘ 15 ◘

The Copper Tower

King Acrisius of Argos was the most superstitious man in the world. He saw omens in the moon and stars; if his ships needed wind for their sails he whistled for it, and if he walked under a ladder, he stayed in bed for a week to avoid bad luck.

Now Acrisius had a daughter called Danäe, who was the apple of his eye. "Hello, my flower!" he would say every morning. "Come and give your old father a kiss." But when Danäe was about seventeen, a soothsayer came to Argos, and demanded to tell the king's fortune. He was rather grubby, with a hat hung with rats' tails and a necklace of wild animal teeth. The king was just about to offer him a goblet of wine, and ask what he could do for him, when the soothsayer swayed in front of him and started to dribble and foam at the mouth.

"Beware, oh King, beware!" he wailed. "For your flower will give birth to a seed, and when the seed is grown, then you will die!" And with that, he turned and ran from the room as fast as a leopard.

Acrisius was horrified, but it was quite obvious what the man had meant. So he shut Danäe up in a tower which he covered from top to bottom in copper, so that no one could get in or out. Only a small flap at the foot for food and a small hole in the roof for air were left, and no one could have got through those.

"Now she will never have children," said the king. "And I shall live forever!" But Zeus was passing by as Acrisius spoke, and the king's words made him very angry.

"We shall see about that," he roared in Acrisius's frightened ear. "For only the gods can make you immortal, and I don't think *you* deserve it!" And with that he changed himself into a shower of golden rain and dived through the hole in the roof of Danäe's tower.

Danäe was very pleased to see the pretty raindrops, and they danced and played with her all day long. In due course, Danäe gave birth to a baby boy called Perseus, but Danäe always thought of him as her little rainbow.

Acrisius didn't dare to offend Zeus by harming his grandchild, because he knew that Perseus was Zeus's son. But he knew he had to get rid of him.

So at dead of night he and his soldiers made a big hole in the tower, and dragged Perseus and Danäe out. They were bundled into a large chest, and thrown off the harbour wall into the sea below.

"That way," thought Acrisius, "if anything bad happens I can blame it on Poseidon." And he went back to his palace and climbed into bed.

The chest tossed and tumbled through the waves at first. But Zeus sent some nymphs to carry it through the sea, and soon the chest bumped up against the shores of Seriphos. A very wet Danäe, clutching a cold and crying baby, climbed out onto the shore of the island. Just then, a poor shepherd passed by, and saw her standing there shivering. He took off his cloak and wrapped her and Perseus in it. Then he took them back to his cottage, and they lived there happily for many years until Perseus grew up into a handsome young man and went off on his adventures.

After a rest Atticus and Melissa set off again. Soon they passed through a village.

"Hey! Where are you going?" yelled a boy, running after them.

"I'm off to catch the boat for Delos. Would you like to walk with me for a bit? I'll tell you a story."

"A story? With monsters?" said the boy

Atticus laughed and held out his hand. "What's your name?" he asked.

"Perseus. My father's the blacksmith."

"Well, Perseus, I'll tell you the story of another brave boy called Perseus—one who fought a real monster. And like you, he lived right here on Seriphos!"

16

The Snake-Haired Gorgon

The king of Seriphos wanted to marry Princess Danäe, but she didn't want to marry him at all. So Perseus, Danäe's son by Zeus, went to the king and asked him to find someone else to marry. The king pretended to agree, but what he really wanted was to get Perseus out of the way.

"I suppose I *could* marry another princess," he said. "But you will have to go off and do some very difficult task to make up for my disappointment." Perseus would have done anything to save his mother, and he said so.

"Very well," said the king nastily. "You shall go and kill the Gorgon Medusa for me."

"Never mind, mother!" said Perseus as he told Danäe the news. "Surely this old Gorgon can't be too hard to kill. I'll just sneak up on her somehow, and chop her head off while she isn't looking." But Danäe just wailed harder. In fact she wailed so hard that Zeus himself heard her, and looked down from Olympus.

Now Zeus didn't like the king of Seriphos, and because Perseus was his own son, he decided to give him some help. As Perseus set out on his journey, leaving his weeping mother behind, two shining figures appeared on the road in front of him.

"Hail, Perseus!" said the first, a beautiful woman with an owl on her shoulder. "I am Athene." And she gave him a magic shield, all polished like a mirror.

"Hail, Perseus!" said the second, a cheeky-looking youth with a winged hat on his curly head, and winged sandals on his feet. "I am Hermes." And he handed Perseus a magical sword with the words "*Hard as a diamond though it be, the hardest thing can be cut by me!*" engraved on its blade.

"These will help you against the Gorgon Medusa," said Hermes. "But you need three more magical things if you are to succeed, and they are held by the Nymphs of the North. The only people who know where their house is are the Three Grey Women, who are Medusa's sisters. If you come with me, and do just as I say, I can trick them into telling you the way."

Perseus was so amazed by his good luck that he just stood there with his mouth open. Hermes took his hand, and away they flew together, up up up into the blue sky, on on on till the earth changed to white beneath them and the clouds turned dark and sulky above.

The Three Grey Women were quarrelling when Perseus and Hermes landed behind their hut at dusk.

"It's my turn!" shrieked the eldest, who was thin and wispy with long tangled hair and fingernails like rusty swords.

"No! Mine!" screeched the middle sister, who was dumpy and bedraggled, with ears like slimy grey slugs.

"You can't have them till tomorrow!" hissed the youngest, who was completely bald, with a nose like a vulture's beak.

"They only have one eye and one tooth between them," whispered Hermes, "and they're always fighting over them. Now, while I distract the Grey Women, you go and snatch them, and then we can bargain." He stepped out from behind the hut.

"Good morning!" said Hermes, grinning. And he produced a long feather from behind his back and began to tickle the sisters all over. They laughed so much that the eye and tooth fell out of the youngest one's grasp, and rolled towards Perseus, who picked them up and put them in his pocket.

"Time for business!" said Hermes. "Where are the Nymphs of the North?"

"WE'LL NEVER TELL YOU!" yelled the sisters. Hermes sighed.

"Then we'll just have to drop your eye and tooth in the sea," he said. There was dead silence and then all three sisters began babbling.

"Left at the ash tree ... straight on till Dragon Mountain ... past the Sea of Serpents and it's first on the right."

"Thank you!" said Hermes, soaring into the air with Perseus. "Now catch!" And he took the eye and tooth from Perseus and threw them to the ground. The shrieks and curses followed them for miles.

The Nymphs of the North welcomed Perseus, and gladly gave him the magical leather bag, winged sandals and cap of invisibility which he needed.

"Where are you?" asked Hermes, after he had put them on.

"Up here!" laughed the invisible Perseus from above the treetops. And off he flew to look for Medusa, with Hermes's last words floating up to him.

"Use your shield as a mirror to look at the Gorgons, or you will be turned to stone! And remember, Medusa is the only one that looks human!"

After flying for a very long way, he saw a rocky little island thousands of feet below. There was a beach of snowy white sand on the far side, and fast asleep by a cave in the cliffs lay three monsters. They were covered in gigantic greeny-bronze insect scales, and their long thin golden wings rose and fell as they breathed. Instead of hair they all had snakes growing from their heads, writhing and hissing as they slept.

Perseus looked at them carefully in his shield mirror. Which was Medusa? As the monsters sighed and turned over, he saw that the nearest had the face of a beautiful woman. Perseus landed softly and raised his sword, taking careful aim in the mirror. The sword snickered through the silent air and cut down to the sand beneath, as Medusa's head rolled off her shoulders and landed with a thump at his feet. Quickly he opened the magic bag, which stretched itself to the right size at once, and stuffed Medusa's head inside. He felt the snakes wriggling as he attached it to his belt and flew towards the sun.

At that moment the other Gorgons woke up and found their sister dead. How their talons clawed and scratched the air as they flapped round the island, shrieking horribly and looking for someone to turn to stone. But the invisible Perseus fled hurriedly in the other direction, the Gorgon's head safe at his side.

At dawn the next day, Atticus and Melissa left Seriphos and boarded the boat for Delos. Atticus was pleased at how well the journey was going, although it would be months before they reached Troy.

"That's the way Perseus flew when he'd killed Medusa," he said to Melissa, pointing to the south-east. "There was a terrible storm, and he got blown off course."

"Sounds like a good story for a sailor," said Captain Nikos, who owned the boat. So Atticus told the tale while Captain Nikos steered The Star of the Sea towards Delos.

◪ 17 ◪

The Magic Head

The wind blew and the lightning flashed, and Perseus was blown this way and that, through thunder and clouds and rain, till he didn't know which way was up. He clutched his precious bag with one hand and his cap of invisibility with the other, and prayed to Zeus to save him. But Zeus had sent the storm on purpose.

As soon as Perseus was over the coast of Ethiopia, the wind died, and the sun came out in a sky as blue as delphiniums. Looking down, he saw a great rock. Something was moving on the top of it, and Perseus flew down to have a closer look. There, chained to a post, was the loveliest girl he had ever seen.

"Who are you, and what are you doing here?" he asked as he landed, and took off his cap. The girl screamed as he appeared, but when he had calmed her down, she told him that she was Andromeda, the daughter of the king and queen, and that she had been left as a sacrifice to Poseidon, the god of the sea, whom her mother had offended.

"Run for your life," she said. "A monster is coming to eat me up, and if you stay here you will be killed as well!" But Perseus had fallen in love with Andromeda, and was determined to save her if he could. So he hid behind a rock and waited.

Soon a great roiling and boiling in the sea started, and a huge warty head appeared, with trails of seaweed and slime hanging from it. The monster opened its mouth, and showed its teeth, each one as long as a man's arm.

As Andromeda cowered away, Perseus ran forward with his magic sword and plunged it into the creature's throat. It nearly bit his arm off as it reared away, roaring and pouring blood into the water.

With the monster dead, Perseus cut through Andromeda's chains, and they flew to her father's palace. The king and queen were surprised and delighted to see their daughter alive, and agreed that Perseus could marry her at once. But just then in came the man who had been engaged to Andromeda before she had gone off to be sacrificed. He was furious at the king and queen's decision, and rushed at Perseus with his sword raised. Perseus whipped Medusa's head out of his bag, and in a trice the man was turned to stone.

Andromeda and Perseus returned to Seriphos, but Danäe was nowhere to be found. The king of Seriphos had tried to marry her again, and she had gone into hiding.

"How dare he annoy my mother!" roared Perseus. And he marched into the throne room and thrust Medusa's head into the king's surprised face, turning him to stone at once.

The people of Seriphos were happy, because the king had been cruel to all of them. His stone body was thrown into the harbour, and Perseus and Andromeda were crowned king and queen in his place. Danäe came out of hiding, and the joyful hugging and feasting and laughter went on for weeks and weeks. Perseus soon gave Medusa's head and the other magical things back to the gods. And he was so happy that he vowed never to go on any adventures again.

Atticus waved goodbye to Captain Nikos. "See you on the other side of Delos," he called as he stopped at a little market stall by the harbour. A woman was weighing out olives while a boy and a girl were hanging onto her legs and screaming.

"Stories?" she asked. "I wish you'd take these two off my hands for an hour and tell them a story so I could get some work done!"

"I will," said Atticus, "if you'll give me some olives, and some cheese and a bit of bread."

Atticus and the children sat under a shady olive tree, munching and spitting out stones. Atticus stretched and yawned. "See those sunbeams?" he asked. "Those are what Apollo's arrows are made from." The children wriggled closer and settled down to listen.

◙ 18 ◙

Black Python and the Arrows of the Sun

Long ago, when the world was new and strange, Poseidon created the floating island of Delos. It was shaped like a sock, and completely bare except for one huge palm tree right in the middle. One day the goddess Leto landed on the island, right under the palm tree, panting and shaking with fear.

"Hide me quickly, island of the palm tree!" she whispered. "Hera is angry with me! She has sent a terrible snake after me, and she has forbidden the earth to let me step on her body. But you are not attached to the earth, so perhaps I will be safe here!"

Now the reason Hera was so cross with Leto was because Zeus had fallen in love with her, and that made Hera very jealous. Even worse, Leto was going to have twins, and Hera was determined they should not be born, but should stay inside their mother for ever and ever.

Zeus loved Hera even though he was sometimes a bit afraid of her, and he knew he had done wrong, but he also loved Leto. So he persuaded the other goddesses to invite Hera to a party and give her a most beautiful necklace with jewels that gave off a light like sunshine through leaves. Hera was so distracted by the necklace that she forgot about Leto, and soon the babies were born—a boy and a girl named Apollo and Artemis.

Zeus was pleased with his lovely twins, and he gave them each a magical quiver of arrows and a bow to go with them. Artemis's were as soft as the rays of the moon, and Apollo's were as sharp as sunlight. And after they were born, he fixed the island of Delos to the earth, and covered it with trees and flowers and made sandy crescent-shaped coves along its shores so that his children should grow up with beauty all around them.

Now the snake that Hera had sent to kill Leto lived at a place called Delphi. Her name was Python, and she was black and shiny, with needle-sharp fangs that dripped poison and slime. She was also very clever, because she was an oracle and could see into the future. People used to come from far and wide to ask her advice. Delphi had once been a beautiful wooded slope where nymphs sang and played, but Python had made it into a frightening place, full of echoes and shadows and whispers of grey mist. She lived in a damp dark drippy cave, full of bats and spiders, and her throne was a great rock covered in black moss, with a magic pool beneath it, in which Python saw visions of what would happen.

Zeus wanted to get rid of Python, because she had once been rude to him, so when Apollo grew up, he sent him off in a great silver chariot pulled by ice-white swans.

"Kill her with the arrows I gave you," he told Apollo. "She doesn't like bright light." Apollo landed his swans and crept up the hill towards Python's cave. But as he set foot outside her cave, he heard a great hiss.

"Welcome, ssson of Zeusss! My magic pool told me you would come! Come closer sssoo I can ssseee you. Look into my eyessss!"

In two shakes of a snake's tail, Apollo found himself inside the mouth of the cave, staring into a pair of eyes like polished black glass.

"Closser, clossssser!" hissed the snake. Just then Apollo trod on something that crunched, and looked down. Python's fangs just missed his ear, and he jumped back, drawing his bow, and fitting an arrow to the string as he went.

The cave blazed with light, and the great snake screamed, thrashing her tail so wildly that Apollo was knocked off his feet. The arrow had landed right between Python's eyes, and as she died, her spirit fled down to the Underworld, where she hissed the names of those who were to die each day into Hades' ear.

Now that Python was defeated, the nymphs came back to Delphi once more, and made it a place of light and music. And Apollo built a temple around the magic pool and put his own priestess there so that people can visit to hear the Delphic oracle tell their future to this very day.

The Star of the Sea was waiting for Atticus and Melissa on the other side of Delos. It was crowded with passengers going to Naxos.

"Hello, Atticus," said Captain Nikos. "I told everyone about your tales, and they all wanted to come and hear the famous storyteller from Crete."

"Well," said Atticus. "Then I'll tell you about a nymph."

◧ 19 ◧
The Girl Who Grew into a Bay Tree

The river god Peneus raised himself out of the waters and leaned back on the bank. His long green beard flowed down to his waist, and in his hand he held a wand of sweet flowering bulrush. He smiled as he looked downstream to where his favourite daughter, Daphne, was washing her shiny green-gold hair. He must remember to give her a gift, he thought, for only that morning he had found a posy of kingcups by his bed when he woke up. Daphne knew he loved kingcups. He dived underwater, and went to unlock his treasury.

Daphne was worried. The air was calm and still, and it was a beautiful summer's morning. But the swifts seemed to be calling

49

"Danger! Danger!" as they screamed and wheeled across the sky, and even the clouds of midges seemed to be buzzing a warning. She muttered a prayer for protection to Mother Earth as she washed, and Mother Earth shivered comfortingly in reply. Daphne flicked her hair back as she washed it, and the droplets flew from it like miniature rainbows. Just then a stranger stepped out from the trees near the bank and stretched out his hand to catch the water as it fell. There was a small tinkling sound, and suddenly the stranger's hand was full of tiny jewels that flashed fire.

"For you, my beauty!" said the stranger, smiling and holding them out. "I am Apollo." Daphne shrank back. She had never met anyone like this before, and she was frightened. He was so tall, and so golden, and he carried a bow and a quiver of arrows so bright that Daphne was blinded by their light.

She flung up an arm to cover her eyes, and as she did so, Apollo grabbed her around the waist, and threw her over his shoulder, laughing. He began to run into the woods. Daphne screamed as she felt thorns and twigs catch in her long hair, and she kicked Apollo as hard as she could, and bit his hand, so that he dropped her with a cry of surprise.

Daphne began to run. And as she ran she called out to Mother Earth. "Help me! Save me!"

Mother Earth remembered Daphne's earlier prayer, and sent out her power. Daphne felt her feet slow down, and as she watched, her toes sprouted roots, her legs became smooth green bark, and her arms and head became branches. The hair on her head grew flat and smooth and pointed, and attached itself to the twigs sprouting out of her head. A wonderful warm smell of spice came from the leaves. Daphne had turned into a bay tree.

Apollo was sorry for what he had done, and always wore a crown of bay leaves afterwards, so that he would never forget Daphne. But her father Peneus wept for seven long years at her loss, until his river kingdom flooded and burst its banks with grief.

Captain Nikos's boat lay far below in Naxos harbour as Atticus and Melissa puffed and panted their way over the mountains to the other side of the island, where they would find a boat to Caria.

"Oof!" said Atticus, sitting down on a rock. "What a twisty path—it reminds me of King Minos's labyrinth. Did you know that the only person who ever got out of that labyrinth alive landed on Naxos? I'll tell you about him."

◉ 20 ◉

The Monster in the Maze

The breeze brought the news. First it was a whisper in the trees, then it crept through the gates and blew against the palace windows.

"Theseus has returned!" it said. At first the people did not believe it, for what good luck could come to a city that had been cursed for eighteen long years? But then the palace trumpets blew, and the heralds went through the streets, and the people finally believed that King Aegeus's lost son had come back to them at last.

"Maybe he will stop the monster eating our children," they muttered to one another. "Maybe he is the hero we have been waiting for."

In the royal palace of Athens Theseus looked at the father he had only just found. "You want me to sail to Crete and kill the Minotaur?" he asked. "But why?" King Aegeus pulled at his long beard despairingly.

"For eighteen years King Minos has demanded a terrible sacrifice from us. Every nine years we have to send seven girls and seven boys to be eaten up by his dreadful monster, the Minotaur, otherwise he will send his armies to kill us all. You are strong and clever. If you go with them, you may be able to think of some way of saving us."

Early next morning, a fleet of black-sailed ships set out for Crete.

"Goodbye, people of Athens!" shouted Theseus from the deck. "If I succeed, we will hoist white sails for our return. If the sails are still black, you will know I have failed."

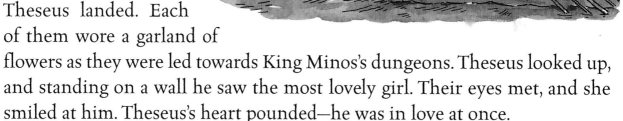

When the ships reached Crete, the harbour walls were packed with faces as the thirteen children and Theseus landed. Each of them wore a garland of flowers as they were led towards King Minos's dungeons. Theseus looked up, and standing on a wall he saw the most lovely girl. Their eyes met, and she smiled at him. Theseus's heart pounded—he was in love at once.

The dungeons were dark and smelly, and that evening Theseus paced up and down as he tried to think of a plan. Suddenly, he heard a whisper.

"Psst!" it said. "Come to the window!"

"Quick! Help me up!" said Theseus to the boy next to him, and the boy pushed him up to the tiny barred opening, where he clung on tightly. Just outside stood the lovely girl!

"I am Ariadne, the king's daughter, and I've come to save you!" Theseus was amazed.

"But how?" he whispered back.

Ariadne handed him something through the window. "I made Daedalus give me this. He's my father's inventor. It's magic string. It can never get tangled up. If you tie one end to your belt, and drop the ball as you go into the maze, you can find your way back by following the thread." Then she handed him a sharp dagger. "Kill the Minotaur with this, and when you come back I will be waiting with your friends and we can escape together. I hate my father for his cruelty, and I want to run away with you."

Soon Theseus heard the clank of armour coming along the passage. He hid the magic string and the dagger in his vest.

"Now then, who's first?" asked a rough-looking soldier. Theseus stepped forward.

"Don't worry!" he said to the children, who were shivering and crying in a corner. The soldier laughed cruelly as he dragged him through the deserted passages.

"In there!" he said, pushing Theseus through a large iron door and slamming it shut. There was a dreadful bellowing noise coming from somewhere inside, but Theseus quickly tied the string to his belt, dropped the ball, and walked forward. The thread unrolled behind him.

The labyrinth twisted and turned, so that Theseus became confused. The roaring got louder and louder, making the floor and walls shake, and soon he could hear words.

"Meat! Meat! Want man meat to eat!" All at once, a monster burst round the corner. It had the body of a man and the head of a bull, and its jaws were dripping with red foam. Theseus ran towards it with his dagger clenched in his teeth, swung himself up on its huge horns, and leapt onto its back. The Minotaur bellowed again and tried to shake him off, but Theseus took his dagger and stabbed it till it was dead. Then he followed the string back through the twists and turns of the maze to the great iron door. It was still closed.

"Let me out!" he whispered, knocking on it softly. And like a miracle, it opened. There was Ariadne, standing with the thirteen children behind her. The rough soldier lay snoring on the floor, a cup of drugged wine by his side.

Quickly they ran through the darkness to the waiting ships. The sails were soon up, and they were sailing away, safe at last!

As dawn rose, they landed on the island of Naxos. Theseus was just about to take Ariadne in his arms and kiss her when a shining ball of light appeared before them. Out stepped the god Dionysius, and snatched Ariadne from Theseus.

"You may not marry her!" said the god. "For Zeus has written her name in the stars, and she is to be my queen!" Theseus knew that gods are not to be argued with, so he bowed his head and walked sadly back to his ships. In fact he was so sad that he forgot to change the sails on the ships from black to white.

Every day King Aegeus stood on the high cliffs of Sounion, watching for his son. When he saw the black sails on the horizon he gave a great wail of despair, and threw himself down into the sea below. Although there was great rejoicing at the Minotaur's defeat, the people wept for their poor dead king. They named the sea in which he had drowned the Aegean in his honour. Theseus became king and ruled Athens well for many long years.

But he never saw Ariadne again. She married Dionysius, and in the end he made her very happy. And when she died, Zeus took her crown and hung it among the stars, so that her name should never be forgotten.

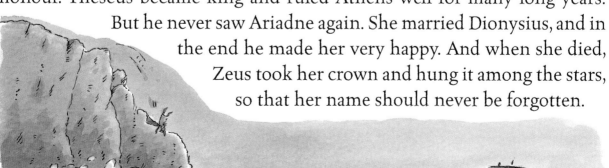

A storm rolled in from the sea as Atticus and Melissa left the small port on the other side of Naxos, boarding the big boat that would take them all the way to Caria. The huge waves and freezing rain made Atticus feel seasick.

Melissa just rolled her eyes and brayed mournfully.

"I know what, I'll tell you about Philemon and Baucis," said Atticus. "It might take our minds off the weather." He pulled a rug over them both and began.

◙ 21 ◙

The Generous Couple

Zeus and Hermes used to stroll through the world, listening at doors and peeping into keyholes. They stood on market corners and hid behind pillars, and everywhere they went it was the same. Cheating and lying, stealing and fighting—and even worse, murdering and killing for no reason at all. No one honoured the gods, and the temples were bare and untidy.

"What ungrateful creatures these humans are," said Zeus. "Let's wash them off the face of the earth and start again. I bet you a dragon's golden hoard that we can't find a single good human being before tomorrow morning, let alone two."

Now Hermes could never resist a bet, so Zeus and Hermes disguised themselves as beggars, and set off at once. In the first village they came to they were pelted with rotten vegetables, in the next it was stones, and in the next they had the dogs turned loose on them. It was the same all over the world. When they had finished running away, they found themselves at the top of a hill, in front of a tiny cottage. Two old people, a man and a woman, were sitting outside in the sun, holding hands.

"Whatever has happened to you?" said the old woman, jumping up. "You poor creatures! Come and sit down while I get water and bandages for your cuts, and then I shall cook a nice big goose for your dinner. Why! you look half starved." The old man went to help her as she bustled about, and soon Zeus and Hermes were sitting down to a wonderful feast, their cuts and bruises all bathed and soothed.

"What are your names?" asked Zeus, as he bit at a bone.

"I am Philemon," said the old man, "and this is my wife, Baucis." As he finished speaking, the gods flew up from the table and revealed themselves in their shining robes.

"You are the only good people in all the world," said Hermes. "So you shall be saved when the great flood comes."

And so they were. Zeus sent a huge flood to destroy all the bad people, and the earth was covered in water for many weeks. Only one spot stood clear of the flood—a small green hill with a beautiful temple on it, and an old priest and priestess dressed in white. Philemon and Baucis lived on happily for many years, and when they were very old, they asked the gods to let them die at exactly the same moment. So Zeus turned Philemon into a sturdy oak tree, and Baucis into a graceful lime. The two trees stood in front of the temple, their roots entwined and their leaves whispering to each other in the breeze. And it may be true that they stand there still.

It was cold and frosty, but Atticus and Melissa were glad to be on dry land after the long sea journey. As they climbed past Mount Latmus they met a shepherd playing his flute.

"Will you give me some milk if I tell you a story?" asked Atticus.

The shepherd was delighted to sit down and listen to a story. "It's boring out here all day with just the sheep," he said. "Nothing exciting ever happens."

Atticus laughed. "I'll tell you a story about a young man just like you," he said. "And it took place on this very mountain."

22
The Man Who Loved the Moon

Endymion the shepherd tapped his fingers. Then he twirled his thumbs. Then he counted the wrinkles on his knuckles. His flute was broken, his knife was blunt, and he was bored bored bored with sitting and looking at sheep sheep sheep the whole day long. His father, Zeus, was the ruler of all the gods, and he was allowed to throw thunderbolts and fight giants. So why was it that the handsomest young man in Caria was only allowed to look after a flock of smelly animals?

At dusk, he set off home, driving the sheep in front of him. Their bells rang sweetly as they walked. Just as he reached the top of the hill, he noticed a beautiful woman standing there. She had the full moon behind her,

and she shone with a pearly light that lit up her long hair and her mysterious black eyes. Endymion stared.

"Who are you?" he whispered, falling to his knees. The woman glided over and took his hands. Raising him up, she looked into his face and smiled.

"I am Selene, goddess of the Moon," she said. "And I will love you forever."

Endymion forgot his sheep and his boredom; he forgot everything except Selene. She took him to a cave on Mount Latmus, and there they spent many loving hours together. But Selene was not happy. She loved Endymion so much that she did not want him to grow old and die. So while he slept, she flew up to Zeus.

"Your son is so beautiful," she said. "Please enchant him so that he can never change, and I shall have him forever!" So Zeus went with her to the cave, and there he enchanted Endymion and put him into an eternal sleep. Every night Selene kissed him as she entered his dreams and in time they had fifty lovely daughters together, each more beautiful than the last.

Atticus and Melissa soon left Mount Latmus behind and travelled up towards Lydia. It suddenly seemed a long way from home.

Just outside the town of Colophon they caught up with a procession walking towards the crossroads.

"Trivia and the children will be doing this at home today," said Atticus sadly as he watched the mayor and his wife lay a pile of eggs and onions in the middle of the road. "We always give the goddess Hecate offerings of eggs and onions in the winter—perhaps she gathers them up and makes a feast for the gods."

Melissa flicked her ear crossly as a spider tickled her. It was trying to weave a web.

"That reminds me of a story about a spider. It happened hereabouts."

23

The Web Spinner

Flickety-thump, flickety-thump went the loom, as Arachne tossed the shuttle from side to side, singing loudly as she wove. Her father had invented a new dye that week, and she smiled as she noticed how well the orange pattern showed up on the cloth.

Colour from carrots,
Patterns from fleece,
Clever Arachne,

Best weaver in Greece! she chanted boastfully. Just then there was a knock on the door. An old woman was standing there.

"Excuse me, my dear," she croaked. "But I couldn't help overhearing your song. I'd always heard that the goddess Athene was the best weaver in Greece, but perhaps I'm wrong."

Arachne sniffed and tossed her curls. "Oh, Athene," she said scornfully. "I'm definitely better at weaving than *her*! Why, I'd beat her any day!"

The old woman began to grow taller and straighter. Her straggly grey hair turned silver and shining. An owl flew in and settled on her shoulder. It was Athene herself, and as she clicked her fingers, a magnificent silver loom appeared at her side. Arachne's mouth dropped open, and the shuttle fell from her hand.

"I think we'd better have a little competition, my dear," said Athene, smiling dangerously. "And since you have so much respect for the gods, then perhaps that should be our subject. Time starts NOW!" She turned to her loom and began weaving so quickly that her fingers flashed faster than fireflies.

Arachne ripped the cloth off her loom, and set up new threads. Then she too began to weave. Soon wonderful tapestries started to appear on both looms. Athene's showed Zeus and Hera, Aphrodite and Artemis, and all the gods and goddesses there were, dancing and feasting in Olympia. They were so realistic that you could almost hear their laughter and songs, and not a stitch was out of place.

Arachne's, on the other
hand, showed all the gods and goddesses in
ridiculous situations. Zeus was sitting in a puddle, Athene herself had
sticky honey trickling down her face, Hermes was sitting backwards on a cow,
sticking his tongue out at Hera. When they had finished, Athene came over to
inspect Arachne's work. Not a stitch was missed, not a colour was wrong. But
when Athene saw how Arachne had mocked her, she flew into a rage.

"Wretched girl!" she cried. "Since you think you're so good at weaving,
you shall do it forever more!" As she said the words, Arachne's body shrank
to a tiny ball, her legs and arms multiplied—and Arachne turned into a spider.
She scurried up the wall and let herself down on a single thread of pure silver,
looking sadly at Athene out of her many eyes. And ever since then, she has
been weaving and weaving and weaving. But never again has she woven
anything that mocked the gods and goddesses of Greece.

There was an old man sitting by the side of a well as Atticus and Melissa turned the corner on their way north to Mount Sipylus. His tall pointed cap had fallen over one eye, and he had a jar of wine beside him.

"Morning," said Atticus. "Any room for me there?"

The old man grunted. "Not from round here, are you?"

"No," said Atticus. "I'm from Crete. I'm looking for King Midas's palace."

"That ruin up the hill may be what you are looking for. Wasn't Midas the king with the donkey's ears?" said the old man.

"That's the one," said Atticus. "I'll tell you the story if you like." The old man sat back to listen.

24

The Golden King and the Asses' Ears

Old Silenus the satyr was a bit wobbly. He'd had a party the night before with some nymphs and now his horns hurt and his hooves were tired, and he needed somewhere to sleep. He noticed a nice comfortable looking flowerbed nearby, and settled himself down for a nap.

King Midas was counting his gold when he heard the commotion. Three guards appeared in the throne room, dragging Silenus between them.

"Found him in the garden, your Majesty," said the captain.

"Asleep in your best violets, your Majesty," said the corporal.

"All squashed they are now, your Majesty," said the private.

Now King Midas rather liked satyrs, so instead of punishing Silenus, he put him to bed and sent a message to the god Dionysius to come and collect him. As it happened, Silenus was a favourite of Dionysius's, so he offered King Midas a reward for his kindness.

"Whatever you like," said the god. "Just ask."

King Midas had a passion for gold. He was very rich, but he had never had enough to satisfy him. "I want everything I touch to turn to gold," he said.

"Are you *quite* sure?" asked Dionysius. King Midas nodded. "Very well then," said the god, waving his hand.

As soon as Dionysius had left, King Midas ran around the room, touching everything. Quite soon the room was a-sparkle and a-gleam with gold. The curtains, the chairs, the table, the walls—everything was made of gold.

"Hooray!" shouted King Midas. "I'm rich!" Just then his servants came in to bring him his dinner. But as he grabbed a piece of roast goat to put in his mouth, there was a clang, and a bit of tooth dropped onto the table. The roast goat had turned to gold. Quickly, Midas poured himself some wine. But as he put it to his lips, the liquid turned to solid gold too.

"Oh dear," said King Midas. "Now what shall I do?" As he spoke, his little daughter ran in to say goodnight. The minute he had kissed her, he backed away in horror, for she had turned stiff and golden in an instant.

"NO!" he cried. "Dionysius, please, take this gift away!" Dionysius stepped out from behind a pillar.

"Tell me what is more precious," he asked. "A piece of bread or a lump of gold? A drink of water, or a golden cup? A child's smile, or a golden statue?" Midas fell to his knees.

"I never want to see gold again," he wept. "Tell me how I can get rid of it!"

"You must go to the river and bathe in it. Then you must pour river water over everything you have touched," said the god. Midas ran to the river at once.

Oh how glad he was when his daughter smiled and laughed as the water ran off her nightdress. Oh how happy he was to eat soggy goat's meat and drink watery wine. He vowed never to touch gold again, and he didn't. But he did do one more stupid thing.

Pan the goat god had boasted that his pipes sounded better than Apollo's lyre, and they had agreed that King Midas was to be the judge. Tootle-toot, went Pan. Plinkety-plink, went Apollo. Now Midas didn't want to offend either god, but Apollo was playing a golden lyre. Midas shuddered as he looked at it, because it reminded him of Dionysius's gift.

"Apollo's lyre sounds like a tinkling crystal stream," he said, "but Pan's pipes sound like the sweetest bird. I award the prize to Pan." Of course Apollo was furious.

"The man's an ass!" he shouted crossly. "And he shall have asses' ears to prove it!" Right there and then large hairy ears sprouted from King Midas's head.

"What shall I do? Whatever shall I do?" he moaned, hiding his head in a curtain. Luckily his queen was very clever, and she designed a special tall cap to cover his ears, so that no one would ever know. The lords and ladies of the court thought the cap was very smart, so they all copied it.

Only King Midas's hairdresser was let into the secret, and he promised never to tell on pain of death. But over the years, the secret became heavier and heavier inside him until it was like a great lump of lead in his stomach.

"I've got to tell!" he groaned. "I've got to!" So he dug a little hole by the river and whispered the secret into it. But the wind carried the secret to the reeds, and the reeds rustled it to the birds, and soon the whole world knew that King Midas had asses' ears. All his subjects laughed at him, but they all still wear the cap his wife invented to this very day.

Frost crunched underfoot as Atticus and Melissa picked their way up Mount Sipylus. A small girl ran up to them.

"I'll show you Niobe's weeping rock for a coin!" she squeaked. Atticus sighed. He'd come here specially to see the rock, but he had no money.

"Will you show me if I tell you a story about Niobe instead?" he asked. The girl's eyes brightened.

"Yes!" she said. "Come on, it's this way."

25
The Queen Who Cried Rivers

Queen Niobe of Thebes looked at her seven handsome twin sons and her seven beautiful twin daughters playing in the palace courtyard.

"Surely they are the most wonderful children in the world, and I am the cleverest mother in the universe to have had them all," she boasted to her husband Amphion. "I'm better than a goddess at being a mother any day—after all, look at silly little Leto. She may have had one set of twins, but I've had seven! I think I should be a goddess too." And she ordered the people of Thebes to put up statues of her in the temples and worship her.

Now gods and goddesses have a nasty way of hearing when humans boast, and sure enough, a swallow flew up to Olympus and told Leto what Niobe had said and done.

Leto called her children Apollo and Artemis to her at once.

"Let us teach this woman a lesson," she said. "Let her daughters be frozen to death by icy moonbeams, and let her sons be roasted by the rays of the sun."

Next morning, when Niobe went to wake her children, all she found in their beds were seven little blocks of ice, and seven little heaps of charcoal. Niobe started to weep. She wept so loud and so long that all the people of Thebes covered their ears to shut out the sound. She wept for seven long years, until the palace was swimming with salt and sadness. Eventually Zeus himself became tired of her crying, and he took her away and turned her into a statue, and set her on the slopes of Mount Sipylus where her father Tantalus lived. But even as a statue Niobe still wept, and the tears of her grief have fallen down the cliffs of the mountain in a great bubbling stream from that day to this.

67

Not far from Mount Sipylus they reached the coast again. Atticus soon found a small boat to take him and Melissa on the short journey from Lydia over to the island of Chios. As they sailed out of the bay the eastern horizon slowly turned pink.

"Look!" Atticus whispered. "What a perfect sunrise! Just the right time to tell you the story of Eos the dawn goddess."

◉ 26 ◉
The Grasshopper Husband

Eos lived in a palace to the east of the east of the world. The walls were made of mother of pearl, and the doors of rosepetals. The curtains were spun from cloud shadows, and the carpets woven from the softness of sky. Early each morning, Eos got out of her bed and hung her huge fluffy pink pillows out of the window to be blown about by her sons, the winds. Then she drew a bucket of dew from her magic well, and washed herself all over. The sparkling drops flew down to earth, to tell the world that day had come.

One afternoon, Eos woke from a nap in her garden and as she stepped out of her hammock, she looked down to earth and saw a most beautiful young man. His name was Prince Tithonus, and as soon as Eos saw him she knew she must have him for her husband. She put on her best silver slippers and her best dress, and went to see Zeus.

"Well," said Zeus gruffly. "Marry him if you must, but don't come running to me for any more favours. Hera's not in a very good mood just now, and she wouldn't like it. I shall give him eternal life for a wedding present, and that will have to do."

So Eos married Tithonus, and they lived happily in Eos's palace without a care in the world. But although Zeus had given Tithonus eternal life, he hadn't given him eternal youth, and soon Eos found a wrinkle on Tithonus's forehead, and then a grey hair on his temple. Tithonus was getting old.

"Oh my beloved husband!" cried Eos. "I shall go to Zeus at once, and get you made young again." But Zeus was having another argument with Hera and would not see Eos. Weeping, she returned to Tithonus. Gradually, Tithonus got greyer and greyer, and more and more wrinkled. His back bent, and his legs curved, and he shrank and shrank and shrank until he was so tiny he had to be kept in a little basket in case he got lost. His voice became small and shrill, and at last he turned into a tiny grasshopper, creaking his chirrupy song to his lovely wife forever more. Eos remained as young and beautiful as ever, but now the dew she sheds every morning is mixed with tears, as she mourns the loss of her handsome husband, Tithonus.

The paths through the mountains of Chios were steep and wooded and full of rustling noises. Melissa twitched her tail at the huge hunting dogs panting round her feet as their master talked to Atticus.

"Be careful if you walk across the island that way," he said, pointing to a mountain track. "I've seen a bear up there." Atticus shivered.

"Could you and your dogs come with us?" he asked. "I'll tell you a good tale as we walk."

The hunter clapped him on the shoulder with a huge hand. "Just make sure it's got wild beasts in it."

◉ 27 ◉
The Starry Hunter

Orion was strong and brawny, with muscles like tree roots, and a beard as black as midnight. He carried a club as big as a pillar, and his jewelled sword was sharper than knives. His best friend and cousin was Artemis the huntress, and they used to run together through the woods and fields with their pack of dogs, hunting anything which came their way.

Now the king of Chios was a cunning and crafty man. His island kingdom was overrun with wild beasts, and all his cattle and goats and sheep were being eaten up.

"If I call in Orion, and offer him my daughter in marriage, then perhaps he will rid my island of these wretched animals and I shan't have to pay him." He meant to trick Orion into giving him something for nothing. Orion soon agreed to the bargain, because he loved to hunt, and the princess of Chios was very pretty—but what he didn't know was that she was already promised to someone else. For two weeks Orion hunted wolves and bears, lions and foxes, and at last there was not a wild beast left. He brought all the skins to the palace and laid them at the king's feet.

"The marriage will take place tomorrow," said the crafty king. "But now you must get some rest." As soon as Orion had fallen asleep, the king bound him tightly with ropes, and blinded him with a hot needle. Then he dragged him down to the harbour, and threw him into the sea. But Poseidon the sea god was Orion's father, and he sent a great wave to carry him to the east, where Helios the sun god healed his eyes. Orion strode over the waves back to Chios, but the king had seen him coming and fled with his daughter to a secret place.

Orion soon went back to hunt with Artemis on the island of Crete, and she was very pleased to see him. But Artemis' brother Apollo was jealous of his sister's friendship, so he sent a giant scorpion to attack Orion. Orion didn't hear it coming up behind him as he ran with the hunt, and its huge sting flicked out and stung him in the heel. When Artemis turned round and found her favourite cousin dead on the ground, she was furious with her brother. But she forgave him after he helped her to shape Orion's picture in the stars. And he still hangs there in the winter heavens, his jewelled belt glittering next to his sword, the greatest hunter of them all—never to be forgotten till the world ends and the stars fall down from the sky.

The hunter had escorted Atticus and Melissa as far as the boat for the Greek mainland, but his dogs had made them both nervous, and even Melissa was glad to be afloat again.

Atticus hummed to himself as the old lady beside him rummaged in a bag and offered him a dried fig. Atticus thanked her. He was very hungry. He'd been living on bread and olives for much too long, and what he really fancied was one of Trivia's feasts, with jars of good Cretan wine. Perhaps if he told a story about a feast he'd stop thinking about it.

"Do you know the story of Tantalus?" he asked the old lady.

The old lady nodded. "I like a good story," she said. "But speak up, I'm a bit deaf!"

▣ 28 ▣
The Terrible Feast

Once every month Zeus's son Tantalus went up to Olympus to feast with his father and the other gods.

"How magnificent!" he thought every time he went into the golden banqueting hall.

"How delicious!" he thought every time he tasted a new and amazing dish.

One day Tantalus decided to have his own feast. "I shall invite all the gods, and it will be the best feast ever given on the earth," he said. He sat down at a big table and began to plan. He ordered flowers and garlands, he ordered golden plates and cups set with precious stones. He ordered linen cloths for the tables, and velvet cushions for the floor. He ordered dancing girls and flute-players and the best singers in Asia Minor to entertain his guests.

"But what shall I give them to eat?" he asked himself, scratching his head. "The main course must be something they have never eaten before, and it must be the most precious food in the whole world." Tantalus thought and thought, but nothing seemed good enough for the gods to eat. Then he had an idea. It was a terrible idea.

"My son Pelops is the most precious thing I have. If I kill him and cut him up and make him into a stew, then the gods will be honoured. And they certainly won't have eaten *that* before." So Tantalus killed Pelops, and cut him up, and stewed him with herbs and wine in a cauldron.

The gods were all talking and laughing and spitting olive stones at each other when the trumpets blew to announce the main dish.

"Smells good!" said Zeus, sniffing. "What is it, Tantalus?" But Tantalus wouldn't say.

"Guess!" he grinned. Zeus took a bite. Athene took a bite. Apollo took a bite. All the gods took a bite. But after one chew, they spat their mouthfuls out onto their plates.

"Tantalus!" they all shouted angrily. "You shall be punished! You have made us eat your own son!" And Zeus bound Tantalus in chains and whisked him down to the Underworld at once. He created a magical pool of water and threw Tantalus into it up to his neck. Then he ordered a magical tree to grow right over Tantalus's head, with ripe fruits dangling from it.

"The water will always be just out of reach of your lips, and the fruit out of reach of your hands," said Zeus. "You shall never eat or drink again till the end of time!" Then Zeus went back to Tantalus's palace and brought Pelops back to life. All the bits of him were still in the cauldron or on the plates, except for one shoulder blade, which had been eaten by a dog. Zeus gave Pelops an ivory shoulder blade instead, and all the other gods gave him wonderful gifts to make up for what had happened to him. The best present of all was a team of magic horses that ran like the wind. Poor Pelops recovered quite well from his dreadful ordeal, and lived a long and happy life. But Tantalus is still in the Underworld, and he hasn't eaten or drunk a single thing from that day to this.

Two days later, as they sailed past the island of Euboea, a boy yelled. "Dolphins!"

Atticus leaned over to look. Seven beautiful dolphins were leaping through the waves by the boat. They turned their heads and laughed then sped away again.

"Oh," said the boy, disappointed. "They've gone."

"That reminds me of a story," said Atticus.

◎ 29 ◎
The Dolphin Messenger

Amphitrite lived in the underwater palace of her father, old King Nereus, together with her forty-nine beautiful sisters. Each day they rode their pet dolphins among the coral and seaweed on the bottom of the ocean, picking up pearls and precious stones that had been polished by the waves till they shone. Every evening they braided their long hair with the jewels they had found, and went to feast with their father in his great hall. Each had her own golden throne to sit on.

One night, after supper, King Nereus spoke to Amphitrite.

"My dear," he said. "As my eldest daughter, it is time you were getting married. I have promised you to Poseidon, the god of the sea, and I'm sure he'll make you very happy."

Now Amphitrite was rather frightened of Poseidon since she had seen him in a temper one day. He had struck his magic trident on a rock, and made a great storm come out of nowhere, and Amphitrite had been swept onto some sharp coral and hurt her arm dreadfully.

"Oh, Father!" she cried. "Please don't make me marry *him*!" And she ran from the hall and leapt on to her pet dolphin, whose name was Delphinus. "Take me away and hide me!" she whispered. And Delphinus did.

When Poseidon heard that Amphitrite didn't want to marry him, he was very sad, because he truly loved her. He looked for her everywhere to try to persuade her to change her mind, but it was no good. She was too well hidden. Poseidon asked cross crabs and flickering fishes, he asked lumpy lobsters and odd octopi—he asked every creature in the sea if they had seen Amphitrite, but none of them had. So finally he went to find Delphinus.

"If you know where your mistress is, and you can persuade her to marry me, you shall have a place in the stars forever," said Poseidon. "I really do love her, you know." Delphinus could see that Poseidon was telling the truth, so he took the message to Amphitrite at once.

She and Poseidon were married that day, and they went away on their honeymoon in a chariot pulled by seven dolphins. As for Delphinus, Poseidon kept his promise, and if you look up at the sky on a clear night, you can still see him swimming among the stars.

It had been a long walk across to Athens from the coast, but Atticus and Melissa had reached the famous city at last! The wooded hillside smelt of the smoke of sacrifices as they stood staring upwards at the Acropolis, and the beautiful white buildings shone above them in the pale winter sunlight. An owl hooted in the trees.

"Athene's messenger," said Atticus. "Let's make an offering at her temple. This is Athene's city, you know. She won it from Poseidon in a competition."

30
The Bee of Wisdom

The great god Zeus was worried. He loved his Titan wife, Metis, because she was very clever and gave him good advice. But Mother Earth had told him that if Metis ever bore him a son, then Zeus would be overthrown. Now Zeus liked being king of the gods, and he didn't want that to happen, so he challenged Metis to a game of shape changing. Metis agreed, and as she turned into a bee and buzzed about the room, he sniffed a great sniff with his right nostril, and sucked Metis up into his head.

There she sat, giving him advice when he needed it, and tickling his brain with her tiny feet when he didn't. It was rather uncomfortable, but Zeus just had to put up with it.

What Zeus didn't know was that Metis was pregnant when he turned her into a bee. Soon Metis got very bored inside Zeus's head, and she decided to make some things for her new baby. She magicked herself a loom and some thread, and started to weave a beautiful robe. Thumpety-thump, clickety-click went the loom, and soon Zeus had a headache.

"Stop that!" he grumbled, but Metis carried on. As soon as she had finished the robe, she magicked herself a little hammer and anvil, and started to make a wonderful silver helmet. Bashety-bash, crashety-crash went the hammer.

"Ouch!" roared Zeus, clutching his forehead. Soon his headache was so bad that he called to his son Hephaestus the blacksmith to help him.

"Hum," said Hephaestus. "You've got something in there. The only thing to do is to cut it out." So he took his sharpest chisel and split Zeus's head right open down the middle. Out sprang a beautiful goddess, wearing a shimmering silver robe and a winged silver helmet. She kissed Zeus.

"Sorry about the headache," she said. "I'm your daughter Athene." As soon as Zeus had mended his head (with Metis the bee still safely inside), he invited all the gods to a feast to meet his newest daughter. He was very proud of her, and wanted to give her a present.

"I shall make her the goddess of wisdom and give her a city," he decided. "Perhaps that little one down there will do."

Zeus had just chosen the one place which Poseidon wanted to be *his* city. When Poseidon heard about Zeus's gift to Athene he was very angry. But there was nothing he could do to challenge his powerful brother's decision, so he decided to challenge Athene instead.

"Let us have a competition, dear niece," he said. "We shall both give the people of this place a gift, and they shall decide which is the most useful to them. Whoever wins shall keep the city." Athene agreed at once, and they both flew down to the city, landing on the flat rock the people called the Acropolis.

"My people of Poseidia!" cried Poseidon. "See what I give you!" And he struck a rock with his trident. A stream of water gushed out and the people rushed forward to taste it.

"Ugh!" they said, spitting and coughing. "What horrible salty water! This is no good to us at all!"

"My people of Athens!" cried Athene. "See what I give you!" And she pointed her finger at the ground. Up rose a beautiful tree, with silvery leaves and little hard round fruits. The fruits fell into a wooden barrel on the ground, and the people rushed to look in.

"Oh!" they cried in wonder as they scooped out oil and olives. "How useful! How delicious! Thank you, Athene." Poseidon dived into the sea in a fury, and ever since then, the city of Athens has belonged to the goddess Athene.

The bustle of Athens was soon left behind as Atticus and Melissa walked north-west into the woods near Corydallus. They stopped for the night at a tavern and when he had stabled Melissa, Atticus sat down and rubbed his tired feet while the man on the bench beside him stretched and yawned.

"Long day?" asked Atticus sympathetically.

The man nodded. "I'm exhausted. I only hope the beds are comfortable here— I could sleep for a week."

"Better not sleep too soundly," said Atticus. "You know the story about Procrustes? He had an inn round here somewhere."

31
The Robber's Bed

In the far-off days of his youth, King Aegeus had been secretly married to a beautiful princess of Troezen called Aethra. He had had to leave her behind when he went back to rule Athens, but he never forgot her.

"I shall leave my golden sword and sandals under this great boulder, my darling," he said as he kissed her goodbye. "If we should have a son who is strong enough to get them out, then send him to me, and I shall make him my heir."

In due course, Aethra had a son called Theseus (the one who later killed the Cretan Minotaur). When he was eighteen years old his mother called him to her.

"That boulder in the garden is annoying me," she said. "Could you just move it for me?" Theseus always obeyed his mother, so he put his back against the boulder and pushed. It didn't move. He pushed harder. The boulder moved a fraction. He pushed with all his strength. The boulder toppled over and rolled into the valley below with a crash.

Aethra stepped forward, picked up the golden sword and sandals and gave them to Theseus. "These belonged to your father, King Aegeus. Take them to him in Athens. He will know where they came from." So Theseus packed a bag, kissed his mother and set off to Athens.

He had many adventures along the way, but the strangest of all happened near a place called Corydallus, just outside Athens. As Theseus was walking along, he came to a deep wooded valley. It was dark and gloomy, and no birds sang in the trees. The rain dripped from the leaves in heavy drops and soon Theseus was soaked. As night was falling fast, he was very glad to come to a little hut in a clearing with a long bench outside.

"Hey!" he called at the door. "Is anyone there?" At once a strange old man pranced out. He had a great black beard, and huge arms like treetrunks, but his legs were spindly and thin, and he was completely bald.

"Have you come to try my famous bed, young sir?" he said with a cackle.

Now this old man's name was Procrustes, and he was a very famous robber. He offered lonely travellers supper and the use of his bed for the night. Then he killed them and stole their gold.

Theseus was very tired, so he ate a good supper and then lay down to sleep. His feet dangled over the edge of the bed. Soon he was woken by Procrustes singing softly to himself.

Chop the tall ones, make them fit,
Cut them up, then wait a bit.
Poke them to make sure they're dead,
Steal their gold, then make the bed!
Stretch the short ones till they're tall,
Tie them up then give a haul,
Wait till bones go crick and crack,
Put their gold in a great big sack!

Theseus didn't like Procrustes' song one little bit. He had heard the stories about people disappearing around here, and now he knew why. He leaped out of bed and grabbed the old man. "You will never kill another innocent traveller," he cried. And *snicker-snacker-snick* he chopped Procrustes into tiny little bits with the golden sword before he could sing another note.

When Theseus arrived at Athens, poor King Aegeus wept as he saw his old sword and sandals. "My son," he cried. "You are just in time to sail to Crete and save us from the dreadful Minotaur!" So brave Theseus went straight off to Crete without ever getting to know his father properly, and of course by the time he returned, King Aegeus was dead. But that is another story for another time and another place, because now it's time for bed.

Atticus and Melissa had waited for days before they could catch a boat from the mainland to the tiny island of Aegina. Now Atticus had lost his hat. He searched the ground near the harbour.

"Where did I drop it?" he muttered irritably. "I know it's round here somewhere." Just then a little girl came panting along the path.

"Sir, sir! You dropped your hat! I found it by the fishstall!"

"Thank you," said Atticus. "I'm fond of this hat—we've walked a long way together! Sit here beside me while I wait for a boat, and I'll tell you a story all about someone with sharp eyes just like you."

▣ 32 ▣
The Sharp-Eyed King

King Sisyphus Sharp-Eyes they called him behind his back, because he never missed a thing. If there was a missing coin, Sisyphus would be sure to find it. If a child hid his toy, Sisyphus would be sure to have noticed where it was hidden. He was always stalking the streets of Corinth, watching what his people were doing, peering round corners and into windows until the people of Corinth were the best-behaved in Greece for fear that their king would catch them doing something they shouldn't.

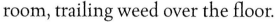

One day, as he was walking outside the city walls, he noticed a very pretty nymph disappear into a cave followed by a cloud of shining dust.

"Aha!" he said to himself. "That'll be Aegina running off with Zeus. I heard he was in love with her. Her father *will* be cross." Sure enough, the next day, the river god Asopus dripped his way angrily into Sisyphus's throne room, trailing weed over the floor.

"Have you seen my daughter?" he asked. "She's disappeared." Sisyphus looked at Asopus and stroked his beard thoughtfully.

"I *might* know where she is," he said. "What's it worth?" After some hard bargaining, Asopus agreed to give Sisyphus a spring of clean water for his city, which was running dry after a drought.

"Now tell me where she is!" he growled, so Sisyphus did. Asopus ran to the cave and burst in, roaring angrily and taking his daughter and Zeus quite by surprise. Zeus had left his thunderbolts at home, but quick as lightning he threw Aegina out of the cave door and right into the Bay of Athens.

"Become an island!" he yelled. Then he turned himself into a bit of the cave wall, so that Asopus couldn't find him.

There was a great big splash as Aegina landed in the sea. Rocks grew out of her body, and earth covered her mouth and eyes, and she spread into a small island all covered with flowers.

It took Zeus a long time to find out who had betrayed him, but when he did, King Sisyphus Sharp-Eyes was made to feel very sorry indeed that he had ever interfered with the ruler of the universe.

A boat had come into Aegina's harbour at last, and it was one Atticus knew.

"Atticus the Storyteller!" bellowed Captain Nikos, as he and Melissa came aboard The Star of the Sea. *"How've you been?" And he clapped Atticus on the shoulder. "Make yourself comfortable while we get under way, and then you can tell me a story."*

As Atticus settled Melissa, he whispered in her ear. "I'll tell Nikos the story of Phaëthon. Nikos seems like a crazy driver too!"

▣ 33 ▣
The Runaway Sun

The Golden Gates of the East flew open, and out galloped Helios the sun god in his fiery chariot. His four chestnut horses snorted sparks of flame from their red nostrils, and Helios had to hold the reins tightly to keep them on the small stony path through the early morning clouds. Up up up the sky they raced, and as they got higher the earth below basked in the warm, bright golden rays that Helios wore as a crown on his head. At the very top of the sky, the path started to curve down, and now the straining horses could see the cool Ocean of the West below. Faster and faster they ran towards their open stables, and soon they were plunging and steaming in the waves while Helios's five daughters prepared golden bowls of hay and oats for them to eat. On earth, night spread her black cloak over all the lands.

Then Helios loaded his chariot and horses onto a golden cloud-boat shaped like a bowl, and set it sailing round the world, back to the Golden Gates of the East. There he slept in his sister Eos's palace until it was time to set out again.

Now Helios had an only son whose name was Phaëthon. He was a spoilt whiny boy, but his father was very fond of him and one day he stupidly made a promise to grant him anything he wanted. The very next morning, just as Helios was about to drive off, Phaëthon came running up to him.

"Father! I want to drive the chariot today! I want to!!!" he wailed in his whingy mingy voice. "You promised me!" Helios knew he had to keep his promise, even though Phaëthon's arms were thin and weedy and not nearly strong enough to control the great chestnut horses. So he got out of the chariot and handed over the reins. When he put his dazzling crown on Phaëthon's head, it was much too big and slipped over Phaëthon's eyes, so that he couldn't see very well.

Just then, Eos opened the gates, and the horses ran through. At first they stayed on the path, but then they realised that their true master was no longer in the chariot. They plunged down to earth, and the lovely green fields

turned brown and burnt as the fiery chariot swept over them. Phaëthon screamed and hauled on the reins, and the horses bolted upwards to the highest heavens. Immediately the earth turned cold and dark, and a covering of ice began to form on its surface.

When Zeus looked down, he saw Phaëthon driving the chariot among the starry creatures of the sky and burning a wide path through the heavens. The swan stretched out her long neck and hissed angrily, the lion lashed his starry tail, and the bull put down his horns to charge. Quickly, Zeus seized a thunderbolt and threw it at Phaëthon. The chariot exploded in a blistering ball of fire, and Phaëthon was thrown out and fell to earth, where he landed in the river Po.

Helios ran to gather the broken pieces of chariot, and took them up to Hephaestus to be mended. His daughters rounded up the horses and took them back to their stables. But they were weeping so much at Phaëthon's death that the river Po became flooded, and several houses were swept away. Zeus felt sorry for the sisters, so he turned their bodies into five tall poplar trees and their tears into drops of amber. If you go to the river Po today, you will still see poplars growing on its banks—and you can still hear their leaves whispering and crying in the breeze for the loss of their beloved brother Phaëthon.

"That was the best story yet!" cried Captain Nikos as they sailed southwards down the coast. " How about some wine, and then you can tell me another."

"I'll tell him about Dionysius," whispered Atticus to Melissa. "Dionysius invented wine, so Nikos should like that!"

◙ 34 ◙

The Secret of Wine

Semele was a mortal princess, with whom the great god Zeus fell in love. He married her secretly, hoping against hope that his jealous goddess wife, Hera, wouldn't find out. But of course she did.

Semele was six months pregnant with Zeus' baby when an old woman came to visit her, carrying a large basket.

"Rattles and toys!" she croaked. "Rattles and toys! Buy my pretty rattles and toys!" Semele was delighted and bought several for when the new baby arrived.

"But where is your husband, my dear?" asked the old woman slyly.

"My husband is the great god Zeus himself. He's too busy doing important things and ruling the world to be here all the time," said Semele proudly. But the old woman didn't seem to believe her.

"Does he glow in the dark? Have you ever seen his thunderbolts? How do you *know*?" she asked. "You should ask him to prove it, just in case he's lying!" Then she went away and as soon as she was outside the palace, she turned back into Hera and flew up to Olympus.

Well, Semele lay awake all that night, wondering and wondering, and the next time Zeus came to visit, she begged and begged him to show her just one thunderbolt.

"Just to prove you really are Zeus," she said, fluttering her eyelashes. Zeus took the smallest thunderbolt out from his bag, but it sizzled so scorchingly that it burnt poor Semele to death. Zeus only just had time to save the baby, which he sewed under the skin of his right thigh.

As soon as Dionysius was born, Zeus hid him away in a beautiful valley, where he grew up with the Maenads, wild dancing maidens who gave wonderful parties for all the nymphs and fauns and satyrs. All over the valley grew vines, covered in juicy purple grapes. One day, Dionysius was bored, so he tipped a lot of grapes into a barrel and started to dance on them. The grapes squelched under his feet, and soon a lot of juice appeared.

Dionysius scooped it into a cup, meaning to drink it, but the Maenads called him to a party, and he forgot all about it. Two weeks later, a delicious smell wafted from the cup as Dionysius walked past. He ran over and drank it down, and that was how wine was invented.

Dionysius went all over the world teaching humans to make this wonderful drink, and everywhere he went, people worshipped him as a new god. Zeus was very proud of him, and even Hera, when she had tried some wine, admitted that it was as nice as ambrosia, and even nicer than nectar. She and Zeus threw a party for him on Olympus, and there he was given his official title—Dionysius, god of wine.

Winter was turning into spring when Atticus and Melissa arrived in the great city of Sparta. Although they had already travelled a long way from Crete, they weren't even halfway to Troy yet. They picked their way through the crowded, noisy market.

"Fine shoes and sandals!" bellowed the cobbler as they passed.

"Not as good as mine!" muttered Atticus. "Now, where's the barber's shop? I need a haircut. Nothing better than a barber's shop for news and gossip!"

The barber was busy sharpening blades when Atticus walked in. "New in town?" he asked.

"Yes," said Atticus. "I'm a storyteller and I wondered . . ."

"Hey!" yelled the barber. "This man's a storyteller. He'll tell us a story while I cut his hair!"

Atticus sat down in the barber's chair and cleared his throat.

35
Rainbow Eggs

The queen of Sparta hung her robe on a bush and dived into the stream. The water was icy cold, but Leda sang as she washed herself. Today something good was going to happen, she could just feel it.

At that very moment Zeus sailed by on a cloud and looked down. He saw Leda's perfect pearly arms raised above her head as she dived, and fell in love at once. Quickly he summoned Aphrodite. She was very sympathetic—love was her business, after all.

"If I turn into a hawk, and you turn into a swan, I can chase you into Leda's arms," she said. "I know she loves birds, and she won't be able to resist stroking your soft white feathers."

The swan flapped frantically up the stream towards Leda with the hawk swooping at its tail.

"Oh! You poor thing!" cried Leda. "I'll protect you. Shoo! Shoo! You horrible hawk!" The hawk swerved away as Leda flapped her hands at it, and the swan nestled into her arms. "What a beautiful creature you are," she said, smoothing its ruffled feathers and kissing the top of its elegant head. "Why, I'm quite in love with you already!"

Nine months later, Leda produced two beautiful eggs. The first shone with bright rainbow colours, and out of it came the lovely Helen of Sparta, who later caused so much trouble to the Greeks and Trojans, and her sister Clytemnestra. The second had a pattern of swirling silver mist, and out of it came the twin brothers Castor and Polydeuces, who became famous heroes. When they died, Zeus took them up to the heavens and made them into twin stars, where they still shine today, hand in hand.

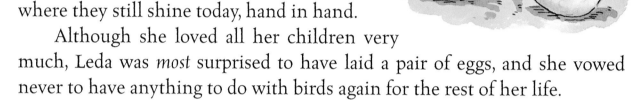

Although she loved all her children very much, Leda was *most* surprised to have laid a pair of eggs, and she vowed never to have anything to do with birds again for the rest of her life.

As Atticus and Melissa walked northwards across the flat plain outside Sparta some men and boys thundered past, each carrying a spear.

"They must be part of the Spartan army," said Atticus. "Look at those horrible faces painted on their shields."

Just then a boy came running up. Tears streaked his grimy face, and he was gasping for breath.

"Whatever's the matter?" asked Atticus.

"I-I'm meant to be joining the army today. I-I'm seven, you see. B-b-but I w-was late, and the other soldiers w-went too fast!" sobbed the boy.

"Never mind," said Atticus. "Dry your eyes and walk with us, and we'll soon catch up with them. I'll tell you a story on the way."

36
War and Strife

The clash of swords and the screams of fighting men rose up to Olympus from earth, and drifted in at the window of the palace of war. Ares, the god of war, was asleep, but as soon as he heard the commotion he leapt off his couch and shook his companion Eris, the spirit of strife. Eris had a golden apple which was so beautiful that everyone wanted to own it. It caused a lot of arguments, which pleased Eris very much—the more arguments the better as far as she was concerned.

"Come on, Eris!" yelled Ares, strapping on his sword as he ran. "Into the battle chariot, quick!" Eris grabbed her helmet and jammed it down over her spiky black hair. She had mean green eyes and a thin sneering mouth which only smiled when her friends Pain, Hunger and Desperation played a nasty joke on some poor human.

Ares's battle chariot had just enough room for two people. Its wheels were armed with dangerous pointed spikes, and the black horses which drew it wore silver armour and had teeth as sharp as daggers. It swept down to earth and hovered above the battle. Ares and Eris yelled gleeful encouragement to both sides, and soon they were in the thick of the fighting themselves. Suddenly a tall soldier with a yellow plume in his helmet came up behind Ares and stabbed him in the calf. All at once Ares began to cry.

"Oh! Oh! Oh! it hurts!" he sobbed. "Someone get me a bandage! Oh! Oh! Oh! I'm going to die!" Now of course gods can't die, because they are immortal and live forever. Ares knew this perfectly well. But he always made a terrible fuss when he was wounded, because he was a dreadful coward at heart.

Eris took Ares back to Olympus, where Zeus gave him some magic ointment and his wound healed immediately.

"Now go away and don't come back!" said Zeus crossly. He disliked Ares because he was so vain and boastful as well as being a coward.

That night Ares gave a feast for all his friends. He sat on his golden throne and boasted about how brave he had been that day, and they all cheered and applauded. But Eris just sat beside him and fingered her beautiful golden apple, and wondered whom it would be nice to upset next.

Atticus and Melissa had delivered the little boy safely to his army camp some weeks before. Sparta was now far behind them to the south, and the hillsides were covered with a spring carpet of blue flowers. The stream rushing down Mount Cyllene looked cool and fresh, so Atticus and Melissa stopped to have a drink. A herd of white cows was coming down the mountain, followed by a dog and a young cowherd.

" Who are you?" asked the cowherd. "Nobody ever comes up here except me."

"I'm a storyteller," said Atticus, " and I'm looking for the cave where Hermes was born. Sit down and I'll tell you the tale."

37
The Baby and the Cows

Maia was the smallest of the Titans. She was always laughing and dancing and picking flowers, and all the gods were very fond of her. But the one who loved her most was Zeus. They married in secret, and because Maia lived in a deep, dark cave on faraway Mount Cyllene, jealous Hera never found out. In due course Maia had a little son, whom she called Hermes. Like his mother, he loved to laugh, and a cheerier, chubbier, cuddlier baby could not have been found anywhere. He was also very clever and loved to play tricks and jokes on his fellow gods. Almost as soon as he was born he sneaked out of his cradle and ran on his baby feet out of the cave and all the way to the Arcadian Meadows, where his brother Apollo's precious white cows were grazing on the soft green grass. Apollo was lying quietly under a tree, singing a little song and dozing in the hot sun.

"Hee hee!" Hermes giggled. "Won't Apollo be surprised when his best cows disappear without leaving any tracks! He'll think a monster has eaten them!" He tiptoed through the flowers and rounded up the fifty fattest cows.

"Quiet!" he whispered as he bound up their hooves with birch bark, and tied straw brooms to their tails so that they would sweep away their own hoofprints. "Come with me!"

On the way home to Maia's cave Hermes felt a bit hungry, so he sat down and ate two whole cows. Then he took the long curvy horns and some other bits of the cows he had eaten, and made a lyre. It was the first lyre ever made in the world, and Hermes was rather pleased with it.

Soon he had hidden the cows in a wood and sneaked back to his cradle, where he snuggled down for a nap.

"You naughty baby!" whispered Maia from her bed. "Where on earth have you been?" But Hermes just burped contentedly. He *had* eaten rather a lot of cow, after all.

At dawn Apollo came raging and shouting into the cave. "Where are my cows?" he yelled. "I know you stole them!" But Hermes just gurgled happily.

Apollo turned scarlet.

"Don't you goo at me, you—you—BABY!" And he scooped him up and whisked him straight up to Olympus, where he burst in on an important meeting of the gods. "This—this—INFANT has stolen my lovely cows, and he won't tell me where they are!" The gods looked startled for a moment, then they burst out laughing. They laughed until they were rolling about on the floor. Little baby Hermes looked so funny standing beside big tall Apollo.

"Oh dear!" said Zeus, wiping the tears from his eyes. "I suppose you'd better have them back. Show your brother where they are, you bad baby!" And Hermes had to do what Zeus said. On the way he picked up his new lyre and showed it to his brother. He ran his fat little fingers across the strings, and a shower of silvery notes pealed out and rang around the valleys.

Now Apollo liked music even more than cows, and the lyre was the most wonderful instrument he had ever heard. In the end Hermes got all the cows as well as Apollo's magic staff, just so Apollo could have the lyre all to himself. And Zeus was so proud of his baby son that he made him the messenger of the gods, and gave him a pair of winged sandals, a magical winged hat and a cloak of invisibility, so that he could flit about the world unseen.

Hermes never stole again, but the gods and goddesses on Olympus always kept a careful eye out for the clever tricks and jokes he played on them every single day.

"We could do with someone like you for our Spring Festival next week," said the cowherd when Atticus had finished. "Why don't you come home with me and the cows? It's only a few days' walk."

The village square was decked with flowers when they arrived, and a group of girls was dancing in the centre. It all reminded Atticus of home. When the mayor heard who Atticus was, he clapped his hands.

"Silence for the great Cretan storyteller!" he shouted.

"Any requests?" asked Atticus. A pretty woman stepped forward.

"I'd like to hear a story about Corinth," she said. "That's where I'm from."

Atticus bowed. "Then I shall tell you the story of how Sisyphus of Corinth tricked the gods for a second time."

38
The King Who Tricked Death

Zeus was very cross with King Sisyphus Sharp-Eyes for getting him into trouble.

"Hades," he said to his gloomy brother. "I want you to drag that wretched king's soul down to your darkest pit, and leave it there for a very long time." So Hades went off to Corinth to do as his brother had asked. Sisyphus pretended to be delighted when Hades arrived.

"How lovely to see you, dear Hades," said Sisyphus. "But why are you here? If you want to take my soul down to your kingdom of Tartarus, you really should have sent Hermes along. It is his job to take souls to the Underworld after all."

Now Sisyphus was perfectly right, and Hades knew it. While he was thinking what to do, Sisyphus whipped a strong chain around his chest and tied him to a large pillar in the courtyard. There was the Lord of Tartarus and the Underworld trussed up like a chicken. Hades was very angry, but there was nothing he could do. None of the mortals could die properly while he was tied up, and so the whole world ran around bumping into the souls which should have been taken down to the Underworld. It was all a dreadful muddle, but in the end the gods forced Sisyphus to untie Hades and let him go.

Hades didn't make the same mistake twice, and as soon as he was safely down in Tartarus, he sent Hermes to take Sisyphus's soul. But sneaky Sisyphus had dressed up as a beggar, and told his wife not to give him a funeral feast, nor to put a coin under his tongue when he died.

When he and Hermes arrived at the river Styx, he couldn't pay the old boatman to take him across.

"Sorry, Charon," he said. "No money." So Hermes had to take him round the long beggar's way. Hades was even angrier than before when they arrived. The rules said that no king could come into the Underworld without a magnificent funeral feast and a golden coin under his tongue. Sisyphus had neither.

"What a terrible wife you have," raged Hades. "You must go back to Corinth at once and teach her how to behave. Really! What a dreadful example she is setting to all the other kings' wives. I shall have no gold coming down here at all at this rate!" So Sisyphus went happily back to Corinth, and kissed his wife as soon as he got there.

"Well done, dear," he said. "We tricked them nicely!"

Sisyphus died of old age after many happy years with his beloved wife. But Hades had his revenge in the end. When Sisyphus finally got down to Tartarus, he gave him a huge boulder.

"Push that up a hill," he snarled. And so poor Sisyphus had to push. Every time he reached the top of the hill, the boulder rolled down, and he had to start all over again. He never did reach the top, and he may well be pushing that boulder still.

By the last day of the Spring Festival Atticus and Melissa were both well fed and rested. They had been staying with the cowherd's mother, and his little twin brother and sister, Phoebus and Phoebe.

"We shall have to move on tomorrow, but tonight I'll tell them another story about a cow, to say thank you," said Atticus, as he filled Melissa's manger with hay.

39

The Hundred-Eyed Watchman

The goddess Hera was sure her husband Zeus was up to something. He had been acting strangely all week, and now she wanted to find out why.

Below on earth it was a beautiful calm sunny day, and as Hera peered suspiciously down from Olympus, she saw a funny thing. A black cloud was moving mysteriously fast along the ground, wriggling and shaking as if something was inside it. Hera dived straight into the middle of the cloud to see if she could catch Zeus with yet another nymph. But when she landed, Zeus was standing there quite innocently, stroking the head of a pretty white cow with a golden halter round her neck.

"My dove!" he said, smiling at Hera nervously. "How nice of you to drop in!" Hera smiled back, but it was a smile full of danger. She knew perfectly well that the cow had been a nymph seconds before. She held out her hand.

"Give her to me at once," she commanded. So Zeus gave her the cow. Hera took the cow—whose name was Io—straight to the secret garden which Gaia had given her as a wedding present, and tied her to a tree. Poor Io mooed miserably as Hera set Argus, the monster with a hundred never-sleeping eyes, to guard her. She didn't like being a cow at all!

Zeus didn't dare rescue Io himself, so he asked his son Hermes to try.

"She keeps me awake at night with her mooing, and besides, it's not her fault that Hera's so jealous." So off went Hermes, wearing a shepherd's tunic, and he skipped right up to Argus and tootled at him on his flute.

"Hello, old monster!" he said. "Still keeping a few eyes on things, I see." Argus grunted. He found being a watchman very dull. It wasn't like fighting other monsters at all. Argus was good at fighting monsters—in fact he had fought the dreadful Echidna, one of the two hideous creatures made long ago by Mother Earth, and killed her.

Hermes began to play a funny little tune on his flute. It was drowsy and dozy and sleepy, and very boring. Soon Argus's eyes began to close. First one, then ten, then fifty, then all hundred eyes snapped shut. Hermes tapped each eye with his magic staff, and Argus fell over dead. Quickly Hermes untied Io, but as soon as she was free she ran home to her father, the river god Inachus. He recognised her at once, even though she was a cow, and rushed off in a fury to kill Zeus. But Zeus saw him coming, and threw a thunderbolt at him.

When Hera discovered that Argus was dead, she wept and wailed. She took his hundred eyes, and stuck them to the tail of her favourite peacock, and there they sit to this day. Then she sent a huge buzzing gadfly after Io. It chased her all over Greece, biting and stinging her till she ran all the way to Egypt. There Hera allowed Zeus to turn her back into a nymph, and the Egyptians worshipped her as a goddess. But Hera made Zeus swear a solemn promise that he would never try to see Io again.

Atticus wished he had never agreed to take Phoebus and Phoebe to their grandmother's village. They never stopped chattering and asking questions as they skipped up the narrow path through the woods.

"How about a story?" said Atticus, who wanted some quiet.

"Yes, please!" said Phoebus and Phoebe.

40
The Chattering Girl and the Beautiful Boy

The woods smelt green and fresh in the spring sunshine, but Hera didn't notice as she tapped her foot impatiently. Echo the nymph had been chattering and yattering for hours about one boring party after another, and now Hera had lost sight of Zeus. She was sure he was chasing some of Echo's friends, judging by the happy squeals coming from the other side of the lake.

"So he said to me . . ." Echo droned on, looking at Hera with a sly little smile. Hera had had enough.

"You're keeping me here deliberately, aren't you?" she said angrily. "Well, I'll soon put a stop to your chatter. From now on you'll only be able to repeat whatever anyone says to you. See how you like that!" And although poor Echo tried and tried to speak, from then on she could say nothing for herself at all.

Now not far away lived a beautiful boy called Narcissus. Everyone was in love with his golden curls, his leaf-green eyes and his pearly white skin. But Narcissus loved nobody back.

"Who could possibly be worthy of lovely lovely me?" he said to himself scornfully.

One day, when Echo was flitting sadly through the woods, she saw Narcissus sleeping in a patch of sunlight. She loved him at once, but how was she to tell him so?

Echo started to follow Narcissus everywhere, hoping that he would say loving words that she could repeat back to him. One day Narcissus was walking through the woods when he discovered a secret glade. The sun poured down through the trees on to a ring of bright green grass surrounding a sparkling silver pool. As Echo slipped behind a bush to watch, Narcissus heard a rustle.

"Is anybody here?" he called.

"*Here!*" replied Echo. Narcissus looked round curiously. Who could it be?

"Come here!" he said.

"*Come here!*" repeated Echo. Now Narcissus was interested. He wanted to see this mysterious person.

"I want to meet you," he cried. Echo had never heard words she wanted to repeat more. She rushed out of the bushes, her arms held wide, ready to throw them around her beloved. But the loss of her voice had made Echo fade away until she was withered and wrinkled and so thin that she was almost transparent.

"Go away! Don't touch me!" cried Narcissus and he ran towards the beautiful pool.

"*Touch me!*" wailed Echo sadly. As she watched, Narcissus seemed to see something in the pool. He reached out to the water, but as he did so, the pool broke up into a million shining ripples.

"Oh!" he cried. "I have found the only one worthy of lovely lovely me at last! But where is he? Where has he gone?" Scornful Narcissus had finally been caught—but he had fallen in love with his own reflection. For days and days he sat by the pool, trying and trying to reach the boy who lived under the silver water while Echo looked on.

"Alas, I cannot have you!" he sobbed, and Echo flitted mournfully round the pool as she repeated his words after him. Soon Narcissus began to fade away too. His golden hair shrank into a small circle of orange, and his pearly skin surrounded it with white petals. Finally, nothing but a small white flower lay on the ground beside the pool. Echo kissed the flower as it faded and died, then she herself became nothing but a wisp of voice hovering in the woods and rocks. And if you shout loudly enough in the right place, Echo will hear you and yes, she will reply. *Yes, she will reply.*

"Peace at last!" said Atticus to Melissa a week later after they had dropped the twins off with their grandmother. "I've never met a noisier pair of six-year-olds!"

As the moon rose over the woods of Arcadia, they settled down for the night by a pool. Just then, a great stag walked out of the trees. His coat was silver in the moonlight. As he put his head down to drink, a single hound bayed in the distance. In an instant the stag had gone.

"It's like the story of Artemis and Actaeon," whispered Atticus.

41

The Huntress in the Pool

Artemis the huntress stood polishing her great silver bow, while Zeus looked on proudly.

"What was it you wanted me for, dear daughter?" he asked.

"Just a little thing, father," said Artemis. "I love my life in the woods and I love to be free, so please, dear, dear Zeus, don't ever make me marry anyone." Zeus was rather startled, but he wanted to please his daughter so he agreed.

"I shall give you a golden chariot, fifty nymphs to guard you, and a pack of my best hounds, so you may run free through the woods forever."

"Thank you," said Artemis, kissing him on the forehead.

Artemis had a lovely time hunting the deer and the wild boar with her nymphs and her lollopy loppy-eared lemon-spotted hounds. At first the nymphs pulled her chariot themselves, but then Artemis captured four of the five magical hinds who lived on the slopes of Mount Ceryneia, and she trained them to pull the chariot instead. Sometimes Artemis was joined by her best friend Orion, but most of the time she hunted alone.

One evening, when the moon was hanging heavy and golden in the sky, a brave young hunter called Actaeon set out with his pack of hounds to chase a great white stag which he had heard was loose in the forest. Soon the hounds were belling and baying and barking through the woods, with Actaeon hard on their heels. All at once he crashed into a clearing. The moonlight shone on the pool in the middle where a beautiful maiden was bathing. A pack of lemon-yellow spotted hounds sat on the bank behind her, growling. Actaeon stood and stared with his mouth open in amazement.

"Wretched hunter!" shouted the maiden. "How dare you interrupt my bath. No man may see the goddess Artemis bare!" And she scooped up some water and flung it at Actaeon's head. As soon as the drops started to run down his cheeks, Actaeon felt something strange happening to him.

His body thickened and became covered in coarse white hair, his arms and legs lengthened and grew hooves, and his head sprouted a pair of magnificent antlers. Actaeon the stag lifted his head and roared with anguish, as his own hounds leapt on him and tore him to pieces.

"He did make a beautiful stag, but he shouldn't have looked," said Artemis, climbing out to dry herself, as she patted his hounds gently. Afterwards she took them into her own pack, and when they died, she sent them to hunt with Orion among the stars.

Atticus and Melissa plodded on under the rustling leaves, until they came to a bend where two large rivers met. A flock of sheep baaed and jangled their bells as they drank. In the distance sat a shepherd boy playing a set of reed pipes.

"My feet are sore, Melissa, and we've walked a long way since we left home," said Atticus. "I shall dangle my toes in the river and tell you the story of Pan and Syrinx."

42

Reed Nymph

In the wooded mountains of Arcady, where the nights are chilly, and the sunlight falls thin and cool through the still green leaves, there lived a beautiful nymph called Syrinx. Every morning she jumped out of her bed of soft moss, and put on her dress of mist and silken spiderwebs.

Then she picked up her horn bow, and ran through the woods with her sisters, chasing the deer, and leaping over the earth as light as thistledown, and as soft as feathers. Every evening she and her sisters sang and danced with the friendly fauns or swam with the merry river spirits, and later they all feasted on dewdrops and honey nectar by the banks of the river Ladon.

Sometimes, when there were festivals and races on Mount Cronus, she would go and visit her cousins, who were the handmaidens of the goddess Artemis. Since Syrinx was so beautiful, many satyrs and spirits were in love with her, but she always laughed at them and ran away.

"Can't catch me!" she called over one slim shoulder, leaping and darting between the trees. And it was true, none of them ever could.

But one day, as she was coming back from Mount Cronus, singing a sweet song to herself, the god Pan passed by. He had great hairy goat legs and a stubby goat tail, and short twisted horns sticking out of the curly hair on his head. He was very ugly, with a wrinkled face, and a chin that stuck out. When he heard Syrinx's voice, he fell in love with her at once.

He straightened the scruffy wreath of pine cones on his head, and lolloped towards her.

"O beautiful nymph," he shouted in his harsh rasping voice. "Come and marry me! I will give you fire-gold and emeralds from the forge of Hephaestus. I will clothe you in the silk of the sunrise, and make you a lyre of phoenix feathers if only you will come away with me and sing me to sleep every night!"

Syrinx looked at him and giggled. He really was very hideous. And besides, she didn't want to marry a goaty old god. She wanted to be free to sing and run and play with her sisters in the woods. So she stuck her tongue out and wiggled her bottom at him rudely.

"Silly old Pan!" she cried. "Who'd marry you?" And then she ran away.

Now everyone knows it doesn't do to be rude to a god. And silly Syrinx had just been very rude indeed. So Pan lost his temper.

"Wretched nymph!" he roared. "Just you wait! I shall catch you and keep you chained up for ever and ever if you don't do as I ask!"

Pan began to run after Syrinx on his strong goaty legs, and soon he began to gain. Syrinx dodged and darted between tree trunks, and over rocks, and under branches, but it was no good. She could hear Pan's hot breath panting as he came closer and closer. She began to be very afraid, and as she approached the river Ladon, she cried out to her friends the river-spirits to save her.

Pan caught up with the terrified Syrinx as she fell gasping at the water's edge, but as he reached out to grasp her arm, the river spirits transformed her, and Pan was left holding nothing but a bundle of marsh reeds in his hand.

As Pan looked down at all that was left of the beautiful nymph, a little puff of wind blew through the reeds in his fingers and set them singing.

Pan was enchanted by the sweetness of the music. He cut the reeds into unequal lengths, and bound them together with wax and gossamer.

"Now we shall really be together for always, lovely Syrinx," he said. "I shall carry you next to my heart forever, and you shall talk to me, and sing to me when I am sad!"

Pan taught his friends the shepherds to make pipes just like his, and to play them to their sheep, so that the beautiful voice of Syrinx the nymph should never be forgotten in the land of Greece.

Mount Cronus loomed distant and black against the sunset as Atticus knocked at the door of a cottage.

"Who's there?" called a cracked old voice.

"My name is Atticus the Storyteller. My donkey and I need a bite to eat and a bit of straw to lie on for the night in exchange for a tale or two." The door opened and a very old lady hobbled out.

"Come in," she said. "I'll be glad of the company."

After Atticus had settled Melissa and eaten a big dish of olives and bread with some white cheese, he asked the old lady what story she would like.

"I'm getting near my life's end, dearie," she said, looking down at her wrinkled hands. "So tell me the story of the spinner and the weaver and the cutter of threads. I'm a weaver myself."

43
The Cloth of Life

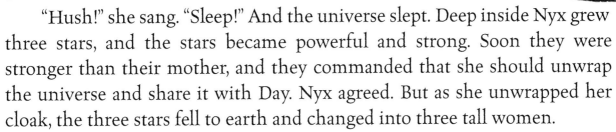

In the time before time, Nyx the goddess of Night spread her great cloak around the universe and held it close.

"Hush!" she sang. "Sleep!" And the universe slept. Deep inside Nyx grew three stars, and the stars became powerful and strong. Soon they were stronger than their mother, and they commanded that she should unwrap the universe and share it with Day. Nyx agreed. But as she unwrapped her cloak, the three stars fell to earth and changed into three tall women.

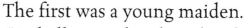

The first was a young maiden.

"I shall spin the threads of life," she sang as she twirled her spindle. "I shall spin the red thread of anger and the blue thread of calm, the white thread of peace and joy and the black thread of despair." And she set to work at once.

The second was a beautiful woman.

"I shall decide the length of the threads of life," she sang as she took out a measuring tape. "I shall measure up heroes who live short lives and cowards who live long. I shall decide when death will come knocking on the doors of kings and commoners, priests and princes, beggars and basketmakers." And she set to work at once.

The third was an old, withered crone.

"I shall cut the threads of life," she sang as she opened a great pair of shears. "I shall snip the lives of all men and women, old and young, rich or poor. My scissors will cut every thread when the time is right." And she set to work at once.

The three women came to be known to men and gods as the Fates. They sat together working at their great tapestry of life, and nothing and nobody could persuade them to change or move a single thread. Although the gods gave them precious gifts and men and women prayed to them every day for the life of a child or a loved one, their power was so great that they just went on spinning and measuring and snipping without ever once taking any notice. Their tapestry grew and grew and became more and more complicated as time went by. And it will go on growing till the world ends and Nyx's cloak covers the universe once more.

Next day Atticus sat on the very top of Mount Cronus and watched a snake sunning itself nearby. He could see the sea in the far-distant west, sparkling in the sunshine. An eagle soared overhead.

"You'd better watch out, snake," said Atticus. "He's looking for supper." The snake raised its head, and its tongue flickered, tasting the air. "I wonder what kind of snakes the Furies had in their hair," said Atticus thoughtfully. "Would you like to hear about them, snake?" The snake hissed.

44
The Kindly Ones

When the Titan, Cronus, gave his father Uranus the great wound that sent him running into the outer darkness of heaven, four drops of Uranus's blood fell to earth. One drop fell into the sea and became the goddess Aphrodite, but the other three drops soaked into the rich soil that lay around Mount Cronus. Soon three small mounds appeared. The earth boiled and bubbled around them, until, *pop pop pop*, hundreds of snakes' heads came out of each mound. Finally three fierce-looking women pushed their way out of the heaving soil. Each had snakes instead of hair, a large pair of copper-coloured wings, a whip in the left hand, and a blazing torch in the right.

"Furies!" they cried harshly as they emerged. "We are the Furies!" Then they started to flap their huge wings and sniff about with their long pointed noses, as the snakes on their heads hissed and wriggled.

"We will light up the hiding places of the wicked ones with our bright torches. We will whip them to the ends of the earth and punish them!" they chanted. And with a great whoosh of coppery feathers they rose into the air and flew off into the world.

For many years the Furies chased and killed those who were unlucky enough or stupid enough to break their laws, and sometimes they made mistakes. But eventually Apollo and Athene, who were tired of the bloodshed, persuaded them to put down their torches and whips, and gave them a temple to themselves. There they became known as the Kindly Ones, and the people were so thankful to be saved from their terrible punishments, that they gave them presents and sacrifices forever after.

The buildings of Olympia spread out below as Atticus and Melissa came down Mount Cronus. Priests were bustling about under the plane trees as they passed.

"This is where the Festival of Zeus is held," said Atticus. "Every four years, the best athletes in Greece come to compete in the Olympic Games, just over there in the stadium. I expect some of them will be training in Elis when we arrive there tomorrow—the Games are only a few months away." Atticus stopped under a wild olive tree. "I'll sit and tell you how it all started."

45
The Games of the Gods

It was a very dangerous thing to be in love with Princess Hippodamia of Elis. Her father, King Oenomaus, had ordered that anyone who wanted to marry her must first race against the team of magic horses which had been given to him by Ares, the cowardly god of war. If the suitor won, the wedding would take place at once. But if he lost, King Oenomaus would chop his head off.

Pelops (the same one who was put in a stew by his father, Tantalus) had heard of Hippodamia's beauty, and he decided to try his luck. He set off with his own team of magical horses, which had been given to him by the gods to make up for being chopped up and served at a feast by his own father.

"After all my horses came from Zeus himself, so they must be able to beat a team that was given by a coward like Ares," he said to himself.

As soon as he saw Hippodamia Pelops fell in love with her and she with him. But Hippodamia didn't know that Pelops had a team of magic horses too. So she bribed a stable boy to loosen a nut on one of her father's chariot wheels, so that it would wobble and go slowly. She wanted Pelops to win. The stable boy hated King Oenomaus, because his elder brother had been one of Hippodamia's unsuccessful suitors, and had had his head chopped off by the king. So instead of loosening just one nut, he took them all out, and replaced them with wax ones.

"Serve him right if he dies!" he thought with a nasty grin.

The red flag dipped, and the horses raced off. At first they were evenly matched, and the chariots hurtled neck and neck round the course.

But soon Pelops began to draw ahead, and King Oenomaus's chariot began to wobble as the wax nuts melted. There was an ear-splitting screech of metal as the chariot flew apart, and the king was thrown to the ground. As Pelops drew up, Hippodamia began to cry and to shake the stable boy, who was standing beside her.

"Wretched wretch! I only asked you to loosen a little nut, so my beloved Pelops would win. Now my father is dead!" she wailed. The stable boy wriggled out of her grip and ran backwards through the crowd, but Pelops strode forward and seized him. Then he marched him to the nearest cliff and threw him into the sea.

"Before I marry Hippodamia, we shall have a fabulous funeral feast for her father!" he declared. "We shall invite all the kings and heroes, and afterwards we shall hold games at Olympia, with prizes of gold and jewels for the winners."

The gods themselves looked down on the games and declared them to be such a success that after Pelops and Hippodamia were married they announced that they would hold them every four years. And so the Olympic Games were created for heroes and heroines from all over Greece to prove their strength and their skill to gods and mortals alike.

Athletes strutted round the streets of Elis, their oiled bodies gleaming in the evening sunshine, their trainers scurrying behind whispering advice. Although the Games didn't officially start till the first full moon of autumn, stallholders were already setting out souvenirs. Atticus and Melissa strolled along, enjoying the sights.

"What a pity we can't stay for the Games," said Atticus. "Look at that discus thrower! He must be almost as strong as Heracles! Poor Heracles, he did have a hard life. Let's find a shady spot to rest in, and you can hear how his troubles came about."

46
The Strongest Man

There was simply no one stronger than Heracles. He was the son of Zeus and the Princess Alcmene, and the great-grandson of Perseus who had killed Medusa the Gorgon. Even when he was a baby he was so strong that he strangled the two huge spotted snakes the goddess Hera had sent to bite him in his cradle. She hated him because her husband Zeus had run off with his mother.

Heracles' enormous strength meant he was not an easy child to have around a polite palace where people behaved themselves, and didn't run around roaring and shouting and breaking things. When he was learning the lyre, his huge fingers plucked the strings so hard that they broke. When he sang, his great voice cracked and broke on the high notes.

In fact Heracles hated singing so much that one day he gave his teacher what he thought was a tiny tap with the lyre, and killed him stone dead. After that he was sent away to be a shepherd.

Heracles was much happier in the mountains, where he could wrestle with lions and bears and wolves to his heart's content. Soon stories of his deeds spread all the way to Thebes, where even King Creon heard of them.

"I must have this hero for my son-in-law!" he said, and he summoned Heracles to come and marry his daughter Megara. Heracles and Megara were happy together, and soon they had lots of children. Heracles loved them all and used to bring them lion cubs to play with. But one day Hera looked down from Olympus and saw Heracles laughing.

"I'll teach him to laugh!" she muttered, and she sent a horrible black cloud of madness to attack Heracles. As soon as it touched him, he imagined he was surrounded by wild beasts, so he killed them all. When the cloud drifted back to Olympus he discovered that Megara and all his children were dead.

"What shall I do?" he wailed, tearing his hair and beating his great chest.

"You must go to Delphi and ask Apollo's oracle for advice," said King Creon, tears running down into his beard. So Heracles went to Delphi to learn what he must do to make up for the awful crime he had committed.

Now the King of Tiryns at that time was Eurystheus, who was Heracles' cousin. He was jealous of Heracles, because he himself was weak and puny, with arms like sticks, thin yellow legs and a squeaky voice. When he heard that the oracle had ordered Heracles to serve him for ten years, and do ten difficult tasks for him, he was delighted. Hera was pleased too, because Eurystheus was a friend of hers, and she knew she could help him to think up some impossible things for Heracles to do.

So Heracles came to the gates of Tiryns to report to his cousin for orders. For the next ten years he had to do everything that Eurystheus said, but he didn't mind at all. He just hoped that one day he would be able to forget the terrible terrible thing he had done.

Two days later Atticus was still in Elis. He was sitting on the steps of the Temple of Aphrodite, looking into the sunset, when a travelling player sat down beside him. The man was dressed in a strange costume, with a moth-eaten lion skin over one shoulder, and he was carrying a mask.

"Coming to see the play tonight?" he asked. "We're acting the labours of Heracles for the Olympic ambassadors—the one about the oxen. It's the first time I've done it, and I'm a bit nervous, to tell you the truth."

"Would you like me to tell you the story to remind you?" asked Atticus.

"My friend," said the actor (whose name was Glaucus), "that would be fabulous!"

47
Cattle Stealer

King Eurystheus had set Heracles an impossible task. He rubbed his hands gleefully as he summoned his cousin to the throne room.

"I want those nice fat red cows belonging to Geryon," he squeaked. "And I want them in a year and a day!" Heracles sighed. He would have to hurry.

Geryon's island was at the farthest edge of the Western Ocean, and a year and a day wasn't nearly long enough to get there and back. He ran to the edge of the land and dived into the sea. Soon he was swimming strongly westwards. But even after he had swum a long long way, Geryon's island was still not in sight, and Heracles was getting tired. He turned over on his back for a rest, and looked up into the sky. Sailing just above him was Helios the sun god in his golden cloud boat. Heracles swam to the nearest rock and hauled himself out of the water. Fitting a huge arrow to his bow, he took aim and shouted:

"Hey, Helios! Lend me your boat for a bit or I'll shoot you down!" Helios had no choice, so he steered his boat to the rock, and got out crossly, pulling his chariot and horses behind him.

"I'll need it back," he said sulkily. "And mind you don't bump it on anything." Heracles pulled two great craggy boulders off the rock and threw them into the ocean so that he could find his way home. They stuck up above the waves, and sailors in later times called them the Pillars of Heracles. Then he set the sails, and vanished into the west.

At last he saw a huge island in front of him. It was covered in flat grassy plains, on which several herds of fat red cattle were grazing. Heracles landed the boat quietly, and sneaked ashore. As soon as he had set foot on land, a huge two-headed dog rushed at him barking. Heracles wrestled it to the ground and threw it into a bush. He set out towards the cattle, but before he could reach them, he was attacked by a hideous giant who was Geryon's shepherd. Heracles punched him in the head and knocked him over.

Then he dragged him over to a water-hole and pushed him into it. Heracles was just rounding up the last cow when he heard a great roar. Geryon himself was running out from his palace.

"How dare you steal my cattle!" he cried, spit and foam flying from his three mouths. Heracles calmly fixed three arrows to his bow, and shot Geryon in each of his three bodies. *Pluff pluff pluff* went the arrows, and Geryon's spindly legs wobbled as he sank to the ground, quite dead.

The red cattle walked quietly into the boat and Heracles sailed back to the mainland. It took him a long time, as the boat didn't like going the wrong way round the world. Just as he was giving the boat back to Helios, Hera sent a cloud of her most vicious gadflies to sting the cows, and they scattered everywhere. Heracles only just had time to round them up on the last day of the year. He drove them to the gates of Tiryns before dawn the next day and yelled up at the windows.

"Cousin Eurystheus! Here are your cows! I've finished my task!" Eurystheus looked out smiling unpleasantly. Heracles might think he'd finished, but he and Hera had another couple of things for him to do before he was free.

"Oh Heracles! Come here a minute!" he called. And poor Heracles trudged into the throne room once again to hear what his next task was to be.

Atticus couldn't believe his luck. After the play was over his new friend Glaucus had invited him to join the travelling players as official storyteller. First of all they were going to visit some of the places where Heracles had performed his tasks, and then they were walking all the way to Corinth! It was exactly the way Atticus and Melissa had been going themselves.

"It'll be nice to have some company for a change," he said to Melissa. "And we can see all their plays. Tonight after supper they all want to hear the story of the Augean stables. The place they're staying in now is so dirty they can't wait to move out!"

48
The Dirtiest Job in the World

King Eurystheus of Tiryns had just set his cousin Heracles another terrible task. He had got together with the goddess Hera to think of something *really* difficult this time, and he rubbed his hands gleefully at the thought of Heracles' face when he had heard what he had to do.

"A little bit of dirt will do him good," he chuckled.

Augeias, King of Elis, had three hundred black bulls and two hundred red, as well as twelve silver and white bulls which were sacred to the gods. He also had herds and herds of wonderful cows. Their mooing kept everyone in Elis awake far into the night, and the clouds of their breath shut out the early morning sun. Their barnyards and stables were filled with dung to the height of five men, and they hadn't been cleaned out for twenty years. The smell was truly dreadful, and the people of Elis all wore masks over their noses.

Heracles only had a year to clean the stables and barns, and to make the floors spotless enough for King Augeias to eat his dinner off. It certainly was an impossible task.

But Heracles was not going to be beaten by a bit of muck. He sat in the middle of a herd of black and red cows, scratching his head and thinking hard. Suddenly he heard the sound of rushing water, and then he had an idea. Elis was built between two rivers. If he could only persuade the rivers to flow through the barns and stables, they would be clean in no time at all. And best of all, he could just sit and watch.

Heracles worked hard to persuade the two rivers to move out of their courses, but at last he managed. "It's only for a day," he said to the river gods, herding the cattle carefully on to a nearby hill.

Next morning King Augeias and the people of Elis saw a wonderful sight. Two great walls of green water were swirling through the mountains of muck, and washing it away to the sea. Soon the stables and barns were as shining and clean as a spring morning, and that night King Augeias ordered a celebration feast.

"I shall eat it off the stable floor!" he laughed, and he invited Heracles to join him.

When Eurystheus heard of Heracles' success, he flung his crown on the ground and jumped on it. "I'll get him yet!" he vowed crossly as he went to think up another impossible task.

It was days since they had left Elis, and they had walked a long way. Melissa's ears drooped in the heat as she climbed the slopes of Mount Erymanthus, followed by two other donkeys carrying masks and costumes and props.

"Never mind," said Atticus, patting her. "Glaucus says there's a nice cool spring at the top, and you can rest."

After supper, the players lay around the fire, some playing music, others just staring into the embers.

"Come on, Atticus," yawned Glaucus. "Tell us a story to send us to sleep."

"I'll tell you about something that happened just down there by that big cave," said Atticus.

49

The Biggest Pig

"Come here, Heracles," said King Eurystheus. "I've thought up another task. My people tell me that a huge and horrible boar is roaming through the countryside up by Mount Erymanthus. It's as big as a house, and it has tusks as long as lances and sharper than scissors. It's killing everything it sees, and it seems to be rather fierce. I want you to go and catch it for me. And mind you bring it back alive."

Heracles gathered his weapons and wrapped himself up warmly. It was winter, and snow was falling softly as he slipped out of the palace gates. He was rather looking forward to this task, although he was more used to killing boar than capturing them. It took him a long time to get to

Mount Erymanthus, but at last he arrived, and he walked around the snowy mountain, thinking out his plan.

Suddenly he heard crashing and grunting above him, and the enormous boar appeared out of the bushes, and ran into a large cave. His little piggy eyes were flashing red with fury, and his tusks were dripping with blood and foam. The bristles on his back stood up like needles, and he was at least as big as a house, if not bigger.

"Ho! Boar!" shouted Heracles. "Come and fight me if you dare!"

There was a squeal of rage, and the boar charged out of the cave again. But Heracles was too clever for him. He ran off up the mountain like a hare, and the boar galloped behind him. The snow got deeper and deeper, and soon the heavy boar was exhausted. His body sank into the snow and stuck fast in a snowdrift. Quickly, Heracles bundled him into a strong chain net, and then he carried him on his shoulders all the way to the gates of Tiryns.

"Cousin Eurystheus!" he called. "I've got the boar you wanted!" But when Eurystheus saw the sharp tusks and heard the great animal squealing and raging to get at him, he ran inside and hid himself in a large bronze jar which he had ordered to be made. Unfortunately one of his servants had filled it with olive oil. And oh! weren't his best robes sticky and greasy when he finally dared to climb out!

Atticus and the players wandered slowly on through the hilly countryside, stopping to perform in several small villages on the way up to Ceryneia. But soon there were no more houses, and they found themselves on a path through the woods. A herd of deer was grazing in a clearing. One of the hinds looked quite golden in the sunlight, and Atticus pointed at her.

"Heracles caught a deer like that near here," he said.

"Hey!" shouted Glaucus. "Time for a rest and a story! Gather round, everyone!"

50
The Golden Deer

Artemis had four magical golden hinds which she used to pull her hunting chariot. But their sister was even more beautiful. She had been too fast even for Artemis to catch, and so she lived in the woods, where Artemis declared her sacred and under her protection.

King Eurystheus had heard about the famous hind from Hera, and he knew how much it would annoy Artemis if she were caught.

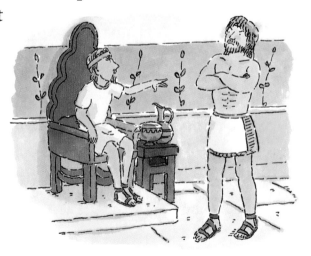

"If I tell Heracles to bring me the hind," he thought, "he will never dare to offend Artemis, and so he will fail. Then I can punish him." He summoned Heracles at once.

"Go to Ceryneia, and bring me Artemis' golden deer," he said. "She will be a nice ornament for the palace gardens."

Heracles went straight to Ceryneia and hid by a pool in the woods. Sure enough the golden deer stepped out of the trees in the evening light and started to drink. Her coat was like sunshine, and her horns shone like fire. As Heracles started to chase after her, her hooves flashed bronze lightning, and she ran faster than the wind. Heracles chased the golden deer for a whole year from Istria to the land of Tauris, but eventually she sank down, exhausted, and Heracles tied her feet together and carried her back to his cousin in Tiryns.

"How pretty she is," said King Eurystheus as he stroked her soft ears and released her among his flowerbeds.

The golden hind only stayed for two days in Eurystheus's palace gardens. Then she jumped over the wall and ran back to the woods of Ceryneia, where she has lived happily ever since.

The journey was not going well. Atticus was sure they were lost. He stumbled over a boulder on the path and sat down heavily. He had terrible blisters.

"Up you get, Atticus," said Georgios, running over to help him up. Georgios was Glaucus's nephew, a boy who helped the actors with their costumes. He was brilliant at designing masks, and Atticus often watched him in the evenings as he sewed and cut and bound together the costumes for the next day's performance.

"You're as strong as a bull!" grunted Atticus as Georgios hauled him to his feet. "But I'll bet you're not as strong as that Cretan bull Heracles had to capture. Just imagine! They say he caught it in the city near my village!"

51

Fire Breather

King Minos of Crete had a problem. A gigantic bull was rampaging all over his island, rooting up the trees with his enormous horns, and trampling the crops with his huge feet.

"I need a hero to deal with this animal," he said to himself. "I wonder if my friend Eurystheus would lend me Heracles."

Eurystheus was delighted. He needed another task for Heracles, and this one sounded perfect. "Bring the bull back here at once," he commanded. "I can use it against my enemies. It will be better than a whole army!"

When Heracles arrived in Minos's wonderful palace, the king was in the middle of a feast. He was very pleased to see Heracles.

"Sit down! Try some of these larks' wings—or perhaps a little simmered turtle egg." Just then a messenger ran in.

"Your Majesty!" he said, bowing and panting. "The citizens of Cydonia are terrified. The bull has driven them all into one house, and he's stamping and snorting and breathing fire from his nostrils. They are trapped!" Heracles leapt up.

"No time for feasting, your Majesty," he said. "I'll be off!" And he grabbed his weapons and followed the messenger out of the door.

The streets of Cydonia were deserted, but from the end of the city came a dreadful screaming and wailing, together with a loud thudding sound. As Heracles ran up, the bull was charging at the door of a large house. His fiery breath had set all the grass alight, and men and women and children were hanging out of the windows, throwing water at it with buckets drawn from the well in the courtyard.

Heracles took a deep breath and bellowed. The bull turned round at once. His little eyes turned scarlet with rage, and sparks flew from his giant hooves. Heracles held out his arms, and as the bull charged at him, he somersaulted on to its back. The bull was very surprised indeed! It ran around the whole island of Crete, trying to throw Heracles off. But Heracles held on with all his might, and squeezed the bull's ribs with his strong legs until it had no breath left, and collapsed on the ground exhausted. Heracles threw a strong iron chain around its neck, and made it swim behind his boat all the way to the mainland. Then he dragged it back to Tiryns, right into the throne room. When the bull could breathe again, it started to bellow.

"Take it to Hera's temple!" squeaked King Eurystheus, quickly hopping into the safety of his bronze jar again. "I give it to her as a gift." But Hera didn't want the bull, so she sent it running all over Greece, until it was so tired that it lay down and died.

Heracles went and looked into the jar. "So, little cousin," he asked. "What would you like me to bring you next?"

There was a huge crowd in the amphitheatre at Sikyon all cheering and clapping loudly as the players bowed and bowed again. Atticus clapped too—he was very happy not to be lost in the woods any more.

Later, he and Glaucus went to an inn with the rest of the actors.

"Feasting is all very well," grumbled Glaucus as they stumbled home late that night, "but not when you have to be up and off early in the morning. Come on, Atticus. Cheer us up with a story."

"Those horse masks you used in the play," said Atticus. "They reminded me of another story about Heracles."

52

The Man-Eating Mares

Now that Heracles had succeeded in so many of the tasks he had been given by his cousin, King Eurystheus, he was feeling quite confident. But the goddess Hera was furious.

"You haven't given him anything difficult enough!" she screeched at the terrified king as he cowered in his bronze jar. "Heracles must fail, and then I shall have an excuse to punish him. All these successes are making his head even bigger than it was before!"

Eurystheus nodded. "I know, great Queen of Heaven," he said. "But he's just so *good* at everything." Then Hera leaned over and whispered in his ear. Eurystheus began laugh. "Perfect!" he sniggered, as he called for Heracles to attend him at once.

Hera had told Eurystheus to send Heracles to capture the four mares belonging to King Diomedes of Thrace. Heracles didn't like horses very much—other animals were all right, but horses kicked and bit, and these mares were particularly nasty. Whenever King Diomedes had strangers as guests, he would treat them to a feast, and if anyone had too much wine and got drunk he would chop them up and feed them to his horses. The mares had got used to eating human flesh, and every time a new groom came near them, they would crunch great lumps out of him with their sharp teeth.

Heracles sailed to Thrace, and when he landed, he tied up his boat and went boldly up to the king's palace. When King Diomedes saw this fine-looking stranger, he smiled a wicked smile.

"A huge man like that will feed my horses for a week!" he thought, as he gave orders for a feast to be prepared, and invited Heracles to join him. Diomedes poured cup after cup of wine for Heracles, but Heracles secretly tipped them behind the silk cushions without anyone noticing. Soon he pretended to go to sleep, and snored loudly. When he felt King Diomedes start to tie up his arms and legs, he leapt up.

"Wretched king!" he roared, brandishing his club. "You shall suffer the same fate you intended for me!" And whacking the king on the head he lifted him up,

and threw him into the brass manger in the mares' stable. The four horses gobbled the king up right away, but as soon as they finished the last mouthful, they became calm and docile, and allowed Heracles to put on their golden bridles and lead them away to his boat.

"Your man-eating horses, dear cousin," he said as they trotted behind him into Eurystheus's throne room. The horses licked their lips and looked at Eurystheus hungrily.

"L-lock th-them in the s-s-tables," stuttered Eurystheus from the safety of his bronze jar. And up on Olympus, Hera looked down and gnashed her teeth in rage as she saw that Heracles had succeeded once again in completing an impossible task.

Loud roaring noises were coming from the rocks above Nemea as they made camp.

"What's that?" asked Agathon, the youngest member of the players.

"It's a mountain lion," said Atticus. "Don't worry, he won't come near our fire."

"Tell us the story of Heracles and the lion, Atticus," called Glaucus. "It'll take young Agathon's mind off tomorrow's performance. He's got to sing a solo!"

53
The Magic Skin

The very first task that Heracles ever had to perform for King Eurystheus was to kill the Nemean lion. This lion was one of the children of the terrible monsters Echidna and Typhon, and it was a most dreadful beast.

Heracles met no one on his way to Nemea—the lion had devoured them all—so he had to search for a long time before he found the lion's cave. When he did find it, the lion was just returning after a day's hunting. He was covered in blood, and flies were buzzing after him as he padded along on his huge paws, swishing his tail like a cat. Heracles hid in a bush and shot several sharp arrows at him. But to his surprise the arrows bounced off, and the lion just yawned and lay down to sleep off his meal. Heracles yelled and charged at him with his sword. It was the strongest sword ever made, but the lion's hide was so tough that it just bent and broke as if it was made of wax. The lion didn't even wake up.

Heracles only had one weapon left—the twisted, knotted club he had had as a boy for protecting his sheep. It was covered in sharp metal spikes, and Heracles lifted it over his shoulders and brought it smashing down on the lion's head. The lion growled and shook his head a little because his ears were ringing, and then he retired into the cave to finish his interrupted sleep.

Heracles looked at the splintered piece of wood in his hands. Whatever could he do? The lion couldn't be killed with any weapon, that was obvious. Heracles would just have to rely on his own strength. He ran into the cave and jumped onto the sleeping lion's back.

He put his huge hands round the lion's neck and began to squeeze. At this, the lion woke up, and began to thrash and roar and roll around the cave floor. But Heracles didn't let go until he was dead.

The people of Tiryns gasped as they saw the lion draped round Heracles' neck. He walked straight into the throne room, and dumped the dead animal at Eurystheus's feet.

"Ugh!" shrieked Eurystheus, running behind a curtain. "Take it away." So Heracles took it away and skinned it with its own sharp claws, and made the skin into armour, which nothing could penetrate. He made the head into a helmet, which he wore whenever he went into battle.

It was after this that the cowardly Eurystheus ordered a great bronze jar to be made, and he decided to hide in it if ever Heracles should bring such a fearsome beast near him again.

Atticus and the others had stopped in Mycenae to watch a juggler while Glaucus found a place to stay. They had been walking for days, and they were all tired of camping on the hard ground. The journey to Corinth was taking a long time in the summer heat.

The juggler threw three brass balls high in the air. One fell, and rolled to a stop at Atticus's feet.

"That's me done for the day," said the juggler as Atticus handed it to him. "It's thirsty work."

"Come and have a drink with us," said Atticus. "Your juggling reminded me of Hera's golden apples. You can listen to the story with my friends."

54
The Golden Apples

Heracles had finished his
tasks in exactly eight years
and a month.

"Can I go now?" he asked. Eurystheus smiled nastily.

"Oh, I don't think so. Not just yet," he said. "Hera says you ought to do
two more things for me, because Iolaus helped you with the Hydra, and you
let the two rivers clean out Augeias' stables for you." Heracles sighed.

Then Eurystheus ordered Heracles to pick him three golden apples
from Hera's secret garden as his eleventh task.

"No one knows the way," he grinned, "except one person. And I'm not
telling you who it is, so there."

Luckily, Heracles already knew that the only person who could tell him
how to get to Hera's garden was Nereus, the Old Man of the Sea. After a long
journey, he tiptoed up to the mouth of the river Po, where Nereus was taking
a nap among the seaweed.

"Got you!" he cried, seizing the god in his strong arms. Nereus woke up
with a jump and turned into a hissing snake. Then he turned quickly into a
lion, a tiny mouse, a worm, a speck of dust and a raging fire. But Heracles held
on, never letting go, and finally Nereus turned back into himself.

"What do *you* want?" he asked grumpily. Heracles told him. "Ho!"
said Nereus. "You want to be careful picking those apples. Only gods can go
into that garden. Atlas lives round there—why don't you ask him to help?"
Then he gave Heracles directions and went back to his seaweed bed.
"And don't come disturbing me again, or I'll turn *you* into something!"
he snarled as he closed his eyes.

Heracles took six months to reach Hera's garden, and he had many adventures getting there. On the way, he passed Prometheus, still chained to his crag in the Caucasus, and still having his liver torn out by the giant eagle every morning. When Heracles heard his groans, he went to visit him.

"Poor old chap," he said sympathetically. "How long is it that you've been here?"

"Thirty thousand years," moaned Prometheus. Heracles took aim at the eagle and shot it dead, then he took his knobbly club, and started to bash and bang at Prometheus's chains.

"It's far too long," said Heracles. "I'm sure Zeus has forgiven you by now." And he was quite right, Zeus had, because Prometheus had given him some very good advice over the years. But he commanded that Prometheus should always wear a chain set with stones from his mountain, so that he would never forget his crime.

When Heracles reached Hera's garden in the farthest west, he found it was surrounded by a high wall. He looked over the top, and there was a beautiful tree, with shining golden apples dangling from its branches in the light of the setting sun. Three nymphs in gauzy dresses were dancing round the tree, watched by an enormous dragon with a hundred heads, which had been set to guard the tree by Hera when her other monster, Argos, had been killed by Hermes.

As Heracles turned to go and find Atlas to help him, he saw a giant hand propping up the sky, just where it curved away on the horizon. When Heracles got nearer, he found Atlas holding up the whole heavens on his shoulders.

"Looks heavy," he said. Atlas nodded, and the sky spilled a few stars.

"It is," he grunted. "Perhaps you'd like to have a go. You look a strong man, and I could do with a rest." Heracles nodded.

"I'll do it if you go and pick me three of those golden apples over there," he agreed. But Atlas looked worried.

"Is that dreadful dragon, Ladon, still there?" he asked. Heracles nodded again. "Well, I won't do it unless you kill him for me. Those hundred heads give me the creeps."

So Heracles crept back to the garden and shot Ladon in the heart with one of his deadly poisoned arrows. The dragon died so quietly that the nymphs didn't even notice.

Heracles swapped places with Atlas, who soon returned with the golden apples.

"You look very comfortable," said Atlas, who was enjoying his freedom. "Tell you what! I'll take the apples to King Eurystheus and you stay here for a bit." A crafty gleam came into his eye. "I promise to come back as soon as I've delivered them!" Heracles could see that Atlas was lying, so he thought he would play a trick on him. The sky was getting very heavy, and he couldn't possibly hold it up for another minute.

"I'll need a pad for my shoulders, then," Heracles said quickly. "Just hold the sky up a second while I run and get one." Atlas put the apples on the ground and shouldered his burden once more. "Sorry, Atlas," said Heracles. "But I really have to go now!" And picking up the apples, he ran off as fast as he could, with Atlas's roars ringing in his ears.

Eurystheus was amazed when he saw the golden apples.

"I can't keep them here," he blustered. "Take them away—they're terribly dangerous!" So Heracles went to find Athene, who took the apples back to Hera's garden and hung them on the tree again. And there they hang to this day, sparkling in the sunset light as the three nymphs dance and play around them.

"Three jars of wine, six obols' worth of olives, ten loaves of bread, and a whole cheese, please," said Atticus, stopping at a stall in the market square in Tiryns. They were travelling northwards again, and the players needed enough supplies to get them to Corinth.

The woman who served him was tall and fat, with huge brawny arms.

"Phew!" said Glaucus when Atticus came over with his packages. "She was large, wasn't she?"

"Yes," said Atticus. "She reminded me of the Amazon Queen, Hippolyta."

55

The Queen's Belt

King Eurystheus had a daughter called Admete. She was a small, scrawny, scrunched-up sort of girl with a shrill voice and a terrible temper. She was also badly spoilt, and her father gave her whatever she wanted. One day she came to see her father, just as he was climbing out of his bronze jar.

"I want a present," she said rudely. "And I want that stupid Heracles to get it for me." King Eurystheus smiled at her lovingly.

"And what would my sweet girl like?" he asked.

"That Amazon Queen, Hippolyta. She's got a magic girdle that helps her fight. I want that so I can fight all the horrid people in this palace who laugh at me behind my back."

King Eurystheus summoned Heracles at once, and told him what his next task was to be. Heracles couldn't help smiling behind his hand.

The thought of scrawny little Admete fighting anyone was funny. But he had to do as Eurystheus wanted, so off he set for the river Thermodon, where the Amazons lived.

The Amazons were fierce women warriors who liked nothing better than a good fight. So Heracles thought he had better take all his weapons, just in case they were too strong for him. But when he landed his boat, a huge woman came running to greet him.

"Hail, Heracles the Hero!" she said. "We have heard of your great deeds, and our queen would like to invite you to a feast in your honour." Heracles was very surprised, but he went with the woman to the palace to meet Queen Hippolyta.

When Queen Hippolyta saw Heracles she was impressed with his size and strength. He told her all about his task, and she kindly agreed to give him her girdle as a present. Now the goddess Hera had disguised herself as one of the Amazons so that she could spy on Heracles, and when she learned of Queen Hippolyta's gift, she was disgusted.

"So Heracles thinks this is an easy task," she spat. "We'll just see about that!" And off she went to spread terrible rumours that Heracles was going to kidnap Hippolyta and carry her off. This made the other Amazons very angry indeed.

As Queen Hippolyta strode down to the shore the morning after the feast to give Heracles her girdle, the Amazons mounted their horses and charged up behind her, shooting arrows as they galloped. Heracles leapt at poor Hippolyta, seized her by the hair and tore the girdle out of her hand.

Then he fought his way through the whole army of Amazons to get back to his boat, leapt aboard and set sail at once. As soon as he got back to Tiryns, he handed the girdle over to Eurystheus, who ran to find his daughter.

"Here you are, my dearest," he said. But Admete just snatched the girdle without a word of thanks and stalked off to find someone to fight.

A terrible smell wafted from the Swamp of Lerna. Everyone held their noses as they hurried past.

"What was that place?" asked Glaucus as they lit the fire that night.

"That was the swamp where the Hydra used to live before Heracles defeated it," said Atticus.

"I made a brilliant Hydra mask for one of our plays in Elis," said Georgios. "It was really frightening. I like that story, Atticus. Will you tell it to us tonight?"

"The minute we've eaten," said Atticus. "I'm starving."

56
The Swamp Monster

For hundreds of years Hera had been protecting a dreadful monster. She thought it would be useful to have a pet monster, in case she needed it to kill someone. So when Eurystheus was thinking up another task for Heracles, she flew down from Olympus to tell him about her Hydra, hoping that it would kill Heracles with its venomous breath.

Now the Hydra lived in a sludgy, squelchy swamp just outside the city of Lerna. It had its lair underneath a tall plane tree right in the middle, where it writhed and wriggled in and out of the filthy water, hissing and spitting horribly smelly poison from its nine snaky heads. One of its heads had a large lump of gold set into it, and it was this head which was the most dangerous, because it could never die.

When Heracles was told about this task, he was in despair.

"How ever shall I kill it?" he asked his friend Iolaus. Iolaus didn't know, but the goddess Athene did, and as Heracles and Iolaus arrived at Lerna, she appeared beside them in their chariot.

"You'll never do this without some help," she said, "and as Hera is helping Eurystheus, I don't see why I shouldn't help you. Now, this is what you have to do."

Heracles followed Athene's advice exactly. He fired burning arrows at the monster to make it come out, and then held his breath while he tried to strangle it. But the monster tripped him up with its scaly tail, and although he kept cutting its heads off with his sword, more and more kept growing. Then Hera sent a huge crab to help the Hydra, and it nipped Heracles' toes till he shrieked and stamped on its shell, crushing it to death.

Iolaus saw that his friend was in trouble, so he set some branches on fire, and rushed in and burnt the stumps where Heracles had cut the Hydra's heads off. This stopped the new ones growing, and finally Heracles was able to cut the last golden head off. He carried it to the shore, and buried it, still hissing, under a great stone. Then he dipped his arrows in the Hydra's poison, making them so dangerous that the slightest wound from one would kill any living thing.

Because Iolaus had helped Heracles in his task, Eurystheus said it didn't count, and so he made Heracles do an extra task as a punishment later on. Hera was furious that her monstrous pet was dead, and it made her hate Heracles more than ever. She took the crab that had helped the Hydra, and placed it among the stars, where it hangs to this very day, nipping at the heels of any who cross its path in the sky.

They had just left the town of Stymphalus when Atticus's sandal strap broke at last. He stopped to rummage for a new pair in Melissa's pack.

"It seems ages since I sat down and made these back in Crete," he said. "I wonder how they're all getting on. Just think of all the places we've seen already, and how far we've still got to go." He gave a big sigh and Melissa blew through her whiskers.

Just then Glaucus gave a shout and pointed ahead. A flock of white ibises had flown up from the marsh to their right. As they flew towards the sunset, their wings turned pink and gold.

"Perhaps those are the famous Stymphalian Birds," said Atticus as he caught up with the others. "But I do hope not." And he began to tell them all the tale as they walked.

57
Bronze Feathers

After Heracles had caught the Hind of Ceryneia, King Eurystheus couldn't think of anything dangerous enough for him to do. Then a messenger came from the people of a village called Stymphalus, to say that they had been invaded by a flock of dreadful birds, which had flown down from the north, and had settled in the nearby marsh. They had sharp feathers of bronze which they plucked out and threw at people, wounding them terribly.

"Go and get me some of those bronze feathers immediately. They'll make a nice crown for me to wear at the next feast," ordered Eurystheus, who was vain as well as cowardly. "You can drive the birds away for the villagers as well."

Heracles arrived in Stymphalus at dawn. The villagers took him to the marsh, where the birds were all roosting in a huge flock in the very middle. As the sun rose, it flashed off their bright feathers, and all the villagers ran away in terror. Heracles started to shoot his arrows at the birds, but they were too far away, and the arrows fell uselessly on the boggy ground.

"Looks like you need some help again, my friend," said a voice beside him. When Heracles turned round, there was Athene, standing laughing at him and holding a great big rattle which Hephaestus the blacksmith god had made for her.

"This will make enough noise to scare those birds away forever, and you can pick up some feathers for that stupid Eurystheus when they've gone. If you tread carefully you won't sink much in the marsh, and you can collect your precious arrows at the same time."

Heracles thanked Athene, and blocked up his ears with wax to shut out the noise. Then he started to swing the rattle. *Whirr-a-whirrrr-a-whirrrr-a-wheeee* it went, and the birds rose straight into the air, screeching with terror,

143

and flew off. As they flew, their feathers cascaded down in showers, and the ground glittered as if it was covered with bronze-coloured snow. Heracles picked the feathers up one by one, careful not to cut his fingers on the sharp edges, and put them into a stout sack.

When he got back to Tiryns, he tipped the sack out at Eurystheus's feet.

"Ooh! Lovely!" squealed Eurystheus, grabbing at the feathers as they fell. But he was soon sorry for his greed as he dabbed at his cut and bleeding fingers.

As for the Stymphalian Birds, they never stopped flying till they reached the Isle of Ares in the Black Sea. And there they lived in peace until a ship full of heroes landed there and chased them away, and they were never heard of again.

At last the players reached Corinth. They had soon found work, and now Glaucus was dancing round Melissa.

"They liked us, Atticus! The Council of Corinth has offered us a permanent post at the amphitheatre!" he shouted. "I can send for my wife and children, and we can get a little house."

"This calls for a celebration story!" Atticus exclaimed, clapping his hands. "What would you like tonight? I'm off to find a boat to Calydon early in the morning, so this will be our last night together."

Glaucus didn't even need to think about it. "It has to be Heracles' last task," he said, beaming. And off he went to arrange a magnificent feast.

58

The Guardian
of the Underworld

Heracles' last task was his most difficult yet.

"Go and fetch me the fearsome dog Cerberus, who guards the gates of Tartarus," squeaked Eurystheus from the safety of his bronze jar. He knew Heracles wouldn't be very pleased.

"Very well, you wretched little man," growled Heracles. "But don't blame me if you're so scared when you see him that you don't come out from that jar for a whole *year!*"

The entrance to the Underworld was very hard to find, and Heracles spent a long time looking for it. He found it at last, but he was in a terrible temper as he climbed down the dark dark passages to Hades' kingdom. When he reached the river Styx, he aimed an arrow at the old boatman, Charon.

"Take me across, or else," he shouted, and as he stepped into the wobbly boat, Charon started rowing as fast as he could. The ghosts on the far side twittered and rustled as he brushed through them, and although he stopped to talk to one or two old friends, Heracles was still in a bad mood. Hades himself trembled at the look on Heracles' face when he marched up to the outer gates of the palace.

"Give me that dog," Heracles demanded, pointing at the horrid three-headed dog growling by the gate. Its heads and back were covered with a mane of writhing snakes, its teeth were as long as spears and it had a lashing serpent's tail. Its great round eyes were as big as cartwheels, and redder than rubies.

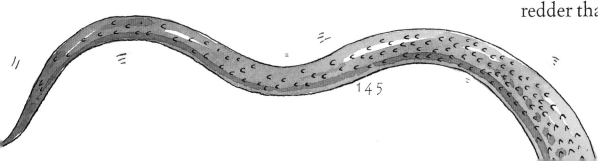

Hades bowed and rubbed his hands together.

"Take him with pleasure," he said. "But you mustn't use your arrows or club."

"Fine!" said Heracles grimly, and he put on the armour he had made from the skin of the Nemean lion. Then he started to wrestle with Cerberus. What a great fight it was. Cerberus bit with all three mouths, and his snake mane hissed and spat, but Heracles hung on and on and on until Cerberus gave up and lay down, all four paws pointing to the dark sky above. Heracles dragged him up to earth, and threw him out of the door of the Underworld into the light of day. Cerberus whimpered as the bright sunshine hit his eyes, and then he started to bark. Great drops of slobber flew from his jaws, and as they landed on the fields, they turned into the poisonous yellow flowers we call aconites.

Heracles took a huge chain made of the hardest diamonds from his pocket, and tied it round Cerberus's neck. Then he pulled him all the way to the palace at Tiryns. Eurystheus took one look at the terrifying beast, and fainted back into his jar. As Heracles had prophesied, he didn't come out for a whole year, and even then he trembled so much that he couldn't eat more than a mouthful at a time.

Heracles didn't know what to do with Cerberus, so he took him back to Tartarus and gave him back to Hades. His twelve tasks were finished and he was a free man at last. Zeus was proud of his fine son, and vowed that one day he should come and live on Olympus. But Heracles travelled round Greece for many more years before that happened, performing greater and greater deeds until there was no one in the whole world who had not heard of Heracles the Hero.

The next morning Atticus and Melissa said goodbye to the players and went down to the harbour. They had to find a ship to take them across the bay to Calydon. As they walked into the busy port, there seemed to be hundreds to choose from.

"If only you had wings like Pegasus, Melissa, then we could fly," sighed Atticus. "But I suppose we'll have to go and bargain for our passage."

As they waited in line to speak to the captain of a likely looking ship, Atticus sat down on the quay, his legs dangling. To pass the time, he decided to tell Melissa a story.

59
The Flying Horse

Bellerophon was the grandson of King Sisyphus Sharp-Eyes, and he had only one dream in his life—to ride on the back of the great winged horse, Pegasus. When the hero Perseus had cut off the Gorgon Medusa's head, the blood from her body had run into the sand. Later that night a beautiful winged horse had been born, and the gods had named him Pegasus, and decreed that he could only be ridden by a great hero. Bellerophon was determined that that hero was going to be him.

When Bellerophon was staying with King Iobates of Lycia, the king asked him a great favour. Iobates had a terrible enemy, the king of Caria, who had a pet monster, the Chimaera. This monster had a lion's body, a goat's head and a snake's tail, and the king of Caria had sent it into Lycia to destroy his enemy's army with its fiery breath.

"If you could only kill the monster," begged King Iobates. "Then my poor soldiers would be saved, and you would be a great hero."

Now Bellerophon wanted to be a hero very much, but he had no idea how to kill a Chimaera. So he went to consult an oracle.

"First you must catch the winged horse, Pegasus, as he drinks at the Spring of Peirene in Corinth. Then you must tame him with Athene's golden bridle before you can ride him to destroy the monster," said the oracle. Bellerophon was delighted, but how was he to get a golden bridle from Athene? He travelled to Corinth, and lay down by the spring to sleep. But before he closed his eyes, he prayed for Athene's help. That night he had a strange dream. A tall woman with a winged helmet and wise grey eyes took him by the hand and pointed to a bush with spiky green leaves. It was Athene, and underneath the bush was a beautiful golden bridle.

Early the next morning Perseus was woken by the hooting of an owl. He sat bolt upright, and there, right in front of him, was the spiky green bush he had seen in his dream! He ran over to it and pulled out the golden bridle just as Pegasus flew down to drink. As the soaring white wings folded, Bellerophon threw the bridle over Pegasus's head and leaped onto his back.

"To Caria," he cried, and Pegasus sprang into the air and started to fly eastwards. Soon they saw a haze of sooty smoke beneath them, and heard the sounds of fighting. Bellerophon fired arrow after arrow at the monstrous Chimaera until it roared and danced with pain. Then Pegasus swooped low enough for him to thrust a spear with a lump of lead on the end into its mouth. The Chimaera bit the spear in its rage, and swallowed it, and the lead melted in the heat of its fiery throat and trickled down inside its stomach, killing it instantly.

King Iobates was delighted and insisted that Bellerophon should marry his daughter and be king after him. But soon Bellerophon longed to ride Pegasus again. One summer's morning he bridled him, and climbed onto his back.

"Fly, Pegasus, fly! Fly to Olympus so that I may see the gods in their palaces!" he cried proudly. Zeus heard him and was angry. He sent a gadfly to sting Pegasus under the tail so that he reared and threw Bellerophon down to earth. Pegasus himself flew on to Olympus, where Zeus now uses him to carry his thunderbolts around the heavens. But proud Bellerophon landed in a prickly thornbush, and Zeus made him wander the world, lame and blind, for the rest of his wretched life.

The sea was calm, and Atticus and Melissa sniffed the salty breeze as they sailed away from Corinth. Just then Atticus felt a tug on his purse. A small boy was trying to loosen it.

"Oi," said Atticus. "Are you trying to rob me?" The boy looked up with scared eyes. "I expect you're hungry, is that it?" The boy nodded.

"If you promise not to steal again, I'll tell you a story and give you something to eat," said Atticus. The boy promised, and they settled down together on deck with some bread and olives while Atticus told a story.

◙ 60 ◙
The Cunning Thief

Autolycus, son of the messenger god Hermes, lived on the Isthmus of Corinth, and he was a cattle thief. But he wasn't just an ordinary cattle thief—no, he was the best and most cunning cattle thief ever born. His father Hermes had given him the gift of transforming whatever beasts he stole, from black to white, or from white to black; from red to yellow or from yellow to red; from horned to unhorned and from unhorned to horned. Whatever beast he stole, he could always disguise it so that not even its mother would have known which it was.

Now Autolycus lived right next door to King Sisyphus Sharp-Eyes, who had a fine fat herd of cattle which he was very proud of. Every night and every day, a cow or two or a prize bull would disappear from Sisyphus's herd, and although he knew it must be Autolycus who was stealing them because his herds were growing bigger every week, even Sisyphus's sharp eyes couldn't spot how he was doing it.

One hot dusty day, King Sisyphus counted up his cattle and found he had just six fine red bulls and twenty fine white cows left.

"I shall lay a trap for Autolycus," he said to his cowherds, "which will catch him once and for all." And he did. He took each cow and each bull's left hoof and carved the words "*Stolen by Autolycus*" in very small letters inside each one. Then he sat and waited. It rained during the night, and in the morning, sure enough, every last one of his cows and bulls had disappeared.

Calling on his friends as witnesses, he followed the trail of marked footprints through the mud and right to the door of Autolycus's house.

"Caught you at last, thief!" he cried. And Autolycus had to give all Sisyphus's cattle back to him. As Autolycus was turning Sisyphus's cattle back to their right colours, Sisyphus caught sight of Autolycus's daughter. He fell in love with her, and later she bore him a son called Odysseus, who went on to become a great hero—and even more cunning than his father and grandfather put together!

The Gulf of Corinth lay below as they walked away from the boat and up towards Calydon. The Temple of Artemis shone white at the top of the wooded hill as Atticus and Melissa stopped to drink at a little spring. The thief boy was following close behind them.

Atticus looked round. "Come on," he said. "Let's go up and make an offering to the goddess. I'll tell you about the death of Heracles on the way."

61

The Poisoned Robe

The river-god Achelous was in love with Deianeira, the beautiful daughter of King Oeneus of Calydon. He had the monstrous head of a bull, with a shaggy wet beard hanging down from his chin, and Deianeira hated him. At that time the hero Heracles was travelling through Calydon, and when he saw Deianeira he knew at once that he wanted to marry her. She was so relieved to have another suitor that she said yes to Heracles immediately, but when Achelous heard that she was going to marry someone else he roared with rage.

"Show me this hero," he shouted. "Let him fight me if he wants to marry you!"

Now Heracles knew all about fighting monsters, and he soon defeated Achelous, who slunk away in shame to a cave made of willow branches. Heracles and Deianeira were soon married, and lived very happily until one day they had to go on a long journey to a place called Trachis. After a while they came to a wide river.

"Oh please don't make me cross it," cried Deianeira. "Achelous might come up out of the water and carry me off." Heracles tried to reassure her, jumping across and back in two great leaps to show her that there was no danger. But still she wouldn't cross. Just then an evil centaur called Nessus came running up.

"I will carry you across, pretty lady. You will be quite safe with me!" Deianeira was pleased, but as soon as Nessus had carried her across the river, he galloped away from Heracles, with Deianeira clinging to his back.

"Help me, Heracles," she cried, so Heracles strung one of his magic arrows and shot Nessus through the chest.

"Take my magic blood, Deianeira," whispered the wicked centaur, as he lay dying. "And if you ever doubt your husband, dip his tunic in it and then he will stay faithful to you and love you forever." Deianeira did as he said, and caught the precious blood in a little bottle.

Heracles and Deianeira arrived at the end of their journey, and settled comfortably into the palace at Trachis. But one day Deianeira caught Heracles looking at one of her ladies in waiting, and she became very jealous. That night she dipped Heracles' best tunic in the centaur's blood, and put it out for him to wear the next morning.

As soon as Heracles put the tunic on he began to gasp with pain. Terrible blisters erupted all over his body, and his very bones felt as if they were on fire. Deianeira began to shriek and cry. She had not known that Nessus's blood was poisonous to mortals, and that this was his revenge on Heracles for killing him.

Heracles was in such pain that he tried to rip off the tunic, but it was stuck to his body. He ran out of the palace and plunged into the nearest stream, but it was no good, the waters just bubbled and boiled with the heat. Heracles knew it was time for him to die, and he asked his friends to build a pyre of oak and olive branches. As soon as it was ready, he spread his lion skin on top of it and lay down, after giving his bow and arrows to his friend Philoctetes. Then Zeus sent down a bright bolt of lightning, and Heracles rose up to Olympus on a shining jet of thunder and flame. There Heracles shed his mortal skin, and the gods welcomed him with seven days of feasting and laughter for the bravest hero ever known in heaven or on earth.

Atticus waved goodbye to the thief boy, who had been given a job by the priestesses, then he and Melissa walked quickly away from the temple. A peal of thunder sounded over the mountains in the far distance.

"That sounds like Zeus. Perhaps he's having another argument with Hera," said Atticus. *"I'll tell you about one of their fights. You seem to walk faster if I'm telling you a story."*

62
The War of the Snake Giants

"I won't have it!" shrieked Hera, kicking Zeus in the shins. "I won't have that hateful Heracles living up here!" Zeus twirled a thunderbolt and sent it crashing into a corner of the room, where it exploded noisily. "Listen to me, wife," he shouted crossly. "We have to have him here, or we shall all die." Hera's mouth fell open as Zeus snatched a golden scroll from his desk and shook it at her. "Read this if you don't believe me!" he yelled. "I got it from the Fates ten thousand years ago!" Hera took the scroll and read out loud:

When snaky Giants curse at gods,
The strongest man must rise,
Or gods will die and Heaven fall
Before your very eyes.

Hera looked at Zeus.

"Those awful snake Giants," she said slowly. "The ones who were howling and shouting up at us from earth yesterday and all last week. Do you think Heracles can really save us from them?"

Zeus nodded. "But we'll all have to help," he said.

Such a clanging of swords and breastplates, such a clashing of spears and shields had never been heard on Olympus. Hephaestus' forge was blazing fiery sparks from morning till night as the gods prepared for their great battle with the fifty-legged snake Giants. As the gods charged down from the gates of Olympus to meet them, the earth shook and trembled, and the people cried out and hid.

Now Mother Earth was still very angry with Zeus, and so she had created the snake Giants in a last attempt to defeat him in battle. They were truly awful to look at. Their fearful fangs snapped and bit at the gods, and every time one was killed and fell to earth, it came alive again. The gods were in despair, but Heracles had once fought and beaten the giant Antaeus, who could not die while he was touching the ground. He knew just what to do to defeat the monsters.

"Lift them up!" Heracles cried to the gods. "Kill them in the air, and then throw them down to the Underworld." Immediately, the gods started to do this and soon the battle was nearly won. But the king of them all, a hideous monster, seized Hera, and was about to carry her off and devour her. Heracles seized his club, and snatching Hera to safety, killed the monster and threw it down to join its brothers and sisters in the pit of Tartarus.

Hera was so pleased to be safe that she begged Heracles to forgive her for all the terrible things she had done to him, and she gave him her daughter Hebe for his wife. Ever since then, Heracles has been the gatekeeper of the gods, letting them in and out, and helping them with any heavy loads. Zeus gave him a wonderful warrior's belt, carved with lions, bears and boars, and a magnificent club studded with all the precious stones of the universe. And since Heracles has been guarding the gates of Olympus, no one has ever dared to attack the gods again.

The band of hunters came round the corner just as Atticus was setting up camp for the night. Their enormous dogs, each wearing a studded collar, sniffed around Melissa's heels until she brayed nervously.

"Can we share your fire tonight, friend?" said the leader.

"The forest is for everyone," said Atticus, "and if you give me some of your hare stew, I'll tell you the best hunting story you ever heard."

The man laughed. "It'll be a fair exchange," he said. "Because we make the best hare stew in all Greece!"

63

Brave Huntress

Meleager, son of Oeneus, was a bold fighter and the most famous javelin-thrower in Greece. Seven days after he was born, the Fates had ordered that his life should be put into a log of wood. As long as the log of wood remained unburned, Meleager could not die.

When the goddess Artemis sent a giant boar rampaging through his father's lands, Meleager knew just what to do. "I shall summon all the heroes to a hunt," he declared, and he sent heralds on swift horses all over Greece.

Many heroes and great fighters came to the hunt—Castor and Polydeuces from Sparta, Theseus of Athens, Admetus, Peleus, Jason and many others—as well as a girl-hunter from Arcadia, whose name was Atalanta.

Atalanta had been abandoned on a mountain hillside as a baby because her parents had wanted a boy, and she had been brought up by a she-bear. So she was very strong and fast, and she carried a bigger bow than some of the men did.

Meleager gave a great feast for nine whole days, and then on the tenth day the hunters gathered in front of the Calydonian Woods.

When one of the hunters, Ancaeus, discovered that a woman was to go with them, he was disgusted.

"I won't hunt with a girl!" he said. "She'll get in the way!" But Meleager told Ancaeus that if he didn't like it he could go home—he rather liked Atalanta and wanted to please her.

The hunters set off, armed to the teeth, and soon they came to the boar's lair. Out it charged, killing two hunters at once, and driving a third up a tree.

Left and right it ran, scattering hunters as it went. Javelins and axes and spears and swords were flying through the air in all directions. Only Atalanta remained calm, and fitting an arrow to her great horn bow, she took aim and fired. The arrow hit the boar behind the ear, but it still kept running.

"What a useless shot," sneered Ancaeus. "Watch how a real hunter does it!" But as he swung his axe, the boar knocked him off his feet and he lay groaning on the ground. Atalanta's arrow had slowed the boar down, and soon Meleager was able to throw a javelin at it and kill it.

"You shall have the skin," he said to Atalanta, "for you drew first blood." But at this, all the hunters began to fight and argue about his decision. Meleager's uncles were the worst, and soon Meleager became so angry with them that he stabbed them in a rage.

Now Meleager's mother had been very fond of her two brothers, and when she heard what he had done, she threw herself on the floor and tore her hair with grief. Then she went to the chest where the precious log that contained Meleager's life was kept.

"You shall not live while my brothers are dead," she cried, and she flung the log onto the fire. At once Meleager felt a great heat inside, and soon he collapsed on the ground in a little heap of ashes. His sisters shrieked so much when they saw what had happened to him that Artemis turned them into guinea-fowl. And that is why all guinea-fowl to this day shriek Meleager's name.

Two great eagles circled in the blue sky as Atticus and Melissa watched.

"Did you know that Zeus once found the middle of the earth by using two eagles?"
Atticus said. "He sent one from each end of the heavens, and they met just above
Delphi, where we're going next. That's why we call Delphi the centre of the universe."

As they went on, they passed through a grove of wild apple trees. Melissa
sniffed at them. "Don't eat those," warned Atticus. "Or I shall have a donkey with
tummy-ache. I'll tell you a story about apples instead."

64
The Girl Who Ran Fastest

When Atalanta's father heard about the fame she had won from wounding the Calydonian boar, he regretted abandoning her.

"She's just as good as a boy," he said to his wife. "We must welcome her back into the family at once." Now Atalanta was not very happy that her mother and father had left her on a hillside to die, but she decided to go and live with them anyway.

"It has to be better than a bear's cave," she said to herself.

When she got there, her father embraced her, and promised her jewels and pretty dresses and a pack of fine hunting dogs all for herself. He also told her that she had to get married.

But although Atalanta liked the pretty dresses and the other gifts, she didn't want to get married at all. She liked her freedom. "Father," she said. "I will do as you ask. But any man who wishes to marry me must first beat me in a running race or else let me kill him." Atalanta's father agreed to this condition, and soon princes were queueing up to ask for her hand. Sadly, none of them succeeded in winning her, because Atalanta was the fastest runner on earth.

One day, a prince called Melanion came to the palace. He admired Atalanta very much, but he didn't want to die as the other princes had done. So he prayed to Aphrodite, goddess of love. Aphrodite was always happy to help lovers, so the night before his race, she came to Melanion's bedroom.

"Here are three golden apples," she said. "They are so beautiful that if you drop one of them each time Atalanta tries to pass you in the race, she will stop to pick them up, and you will win."

Melanion did just as the goddess had told him, and he passed the winning post a second before Atalanta.

"Beat you!" he gasped. "Now you have to marry me!"

In time Atalanta came to love her husband as much as he loved her, and they lived very happily. But one day, when they were on a journey, they passed a spring and turned in to have a drink and a swim. The spring was sacred to the goddess Cybele, and as they splashed and played together in the cool water, she looked down from Olympus and saw them.

"How dare you dirty my spring?" she raged, and she turned them into a pair of lions, harnessed them to her chariot, and drove them off into the sky, roaring furiously at their bad fortune.

The journey to Delphi had taken a long time, but they had arrived at last. The grey mossy trees and stones shimmered in the sunlight as Atticus and Melissa approached the mouth of the temple.

"Leave your donkey here," ordered a priestess, "and stand in the queue."

Atticus had made his offerings, and now he was going to ask Apollo himself what his fortune would be in the competition. The temple was very dark when he entered at last, and all he could see through the smoke of the incense was a veiled figure crouching over a great cleft in the rock beneath.

"Please," he whispered, "tell me if I shall be successful."

Good fortune will come

From Cyrene's son,

But your success

Isn't mine to guess

croaked the Oracle.

"Next please," said the priestess. Atticus stumbled out and went over to Melissa.

"I'm glad that's over," he said. "Let's go up Mount Parnassus now. I'll tell you the story of the Muses on the way. They might hear me and bring us good luck."

65
The Boastful Singer

Thamyris the golden-haired harper could charm the birds out of the trees with his playing and singing.

"I can outplay and outsing even the nine Muses," he boasted to his friends.

161

Now the nine Muses were at that time living on Mount Parnassus, and the winds soon brought them news of Thamyris' rash words.

"I shall send for him and challenge him to a songwriting contest," declared the Muse Erato. And each of her sisters declared that they too would challenge Thamyris to do better than they could.

Thamyris arrived on Parnassus, full of his own importance, and strutted up to Erato and her eight sisters. "So which of my brilliant songs do you want me to sing, girls?" he asked scornfully.

"We just want to see if you can sing at all," said the Muses, and each of them wiggled her little finger behind her back. Thamyris opened his mouth and took up his harp. But his golden voice was dumb, his eyes were blind and his fingers could play nothing but jingling jangling noises, with never a tune to be heard.

Thamyris stumbled away in horror, and as he left, he heard the Muses singing more beautifully than the stars. He never sang or harped again.

It was just after that that the nine daughters of King Pierus challenged the Muses to a song contest. But as soon as they began to sing, their voices turned to raucous squawks, and they found themselves hopping and flapping about the treetops. The Muses had turned them into magpies.

"No mortal will ever sing or play or tell stories as well as we do," said the Muses, as they laughed at the nine silly birds. And it is true, nobody ever has.

Atticus and Melissa were heading to Thessaly when they came up behind a young man and woman.

"Give us a hand," said the man as he struggled with his heavy cart. So Atticus tied Melissa to the front and put his shoulder to the back.

"What on earth have you got in here?" he puffed. The woman pointed to a pile of stones set in a rough square by a small field full of green shoots.

"We're building a house," she said. "We're going to grow some vines and make wine. Would you like to share our midday meal?"

Atticus nodded. "And I'll tell you a story afterwards."

66
The Faithful Wife

Alcestis was the prettiest of King Pelias's daughters, and she was a terrible worry to her father.

"Everyone wants to marry her," he said to his wife. "But how am I to choose a husband for her without offending someone?"

"Simple," said his wife, who was a very wise woman. "Give her to the first man who can harness a lion and a wild boar together and drive them round your racetrack. There won't be many who can do *that*!"

Now at that time the god Apollo had offended Zeus, and as a punishment was working as a shepherd for King Admetus of Thessaly. King Admetus was determined to marry Alcestis, and he asked Apollo for his help.

Apollo had been well treated by the king, and so he summoned his friend Heracles to help with taming the wild beasts. Soon Admetus was driving his chariot round and round King Pelias's racetrack, to gasps of amazement and admiration from the crowd.

His marriage to Alcestis took place the next day, but Admetus was so much in love that he forgot to make the proper wedding sacrifices to Artemis. So when he went into the marriage chamber that night, instead of a lovely bride on the bed, he found a nest of hissing snakes. Admetus yelled to Apollo to help him, and soon everything was sorted out. In fact, Apollo had become so fond of Admetus that as a wedding present he got the Fates drunk and made them promise that Admetus need never die as long as he could find someone to go to Tartarus for him when the time came.

Admetus took Alcestis back to his palace, and for many months they lived happily together. But one morning Hermes knocked at the door. "Time to go to Tartarus," he said.

"But I'm not ready," spluttered Admetus. And he ran around everyone he knew, begging them to go with Hermes in his place.

"Sorry, sir," said his soldiers. "Too busy polishing our helmets, sir!"

"Sorry, Your Majesty," said his courtiers. "Someone's got to run the palace."

"Sorry, son," said his parents. "We're not ready to go yet either." Meanwhile, Alcestis had put on her veil and cloak, and slipped out of the door with Hermes.

"I love him so much," she whispered. "Take me instead."

When Alcestis arrived in Tartarus, Persephone was there to greet her. "I think it's a shame," she said. "Hades should send you back at once." But Hades didn't need to send Alcestis back. When Admetus found out what Alcestis had done he was horrified. He sent for Heracles at once.

"Go and fetch her for me," he ordered. "I can't possibly live without her." So Heracles took his club and marched into Tartarus. Cerberus cowered in a corner as he thundered past, and soon he had snatched Alcestis from Hades's grasp, and whisked her back to her beloved husband. Hades was so impressed with her devotion that he let her go, and Alcestis was famous forever after as the most faithful wife who ever lived.

Atticus and Melissa plodded through the hot, dusty Thessalian village. They stopped at a well under a shady olive tree. Melissa drank thirstily, drops of water dribbling from her whiskery chin as she lifted her head. A little girl ran out from the nearby house.

"Grandma says if you'd like to come in out of the heat, she'll give you some bread and wine." Atticus wiped his forehead and followed her thankfully, leaving Melissa to her drink.

"Would your grandma like to hear a story?" he asked.

67
The First Murder

Ixion was loud and unpleasant. He deliberately laid a fiery pit as a trap for his own father-in-law at his wedding feast, and when he fell in, Ixion just laughed.

"Look where you're going next time!" he called as his father-in-law hopped and danced on the hot coals. And he didn't care at all when the poor man was burned to death. This made him the first murderer in the world.

One day Ixion spotted the goddess Hera bathing in a river.

"She's pretty," he thought, and he began to chase after her. Now Zeus didn't like Ixion, and he thought he would teach him a lesson for trying to steal his wife. So he quickly whisked the real Hera away, and put a Hera-shaped cloud in her place. Ixion was too stupid to notice the difference, and so when he caught up with the cloud, he carried it back to his palace. The cloud, which was afterwards called Nephele, soon escaped, and she later had a child who was the father of the whole race of centaurs.

Zeus ordered Hermes to punish Ixion by tying him to a wheel of flame, and rolling him all over the sky until he cried for mercy.

"That will teach *him* not to play with fire and murder people!" said Zeus, smiling grimly. And it certainly did.

The river's cool green water flowed soothingly over Atticus' swollen feet and Melissa's sore hooves as they crossed the ford. A little way away a young boy, dressed in a sheepskin tunic, sat under a tree plucking at the strings of a lyre. "You're good at that," said Atticus, flopping down beside him.

"I know," said the boy. "I'm practising for the great festival at Athens next year."

"I'm on my way to a festival myself," said Atticus. "A storytelling one."

"Go on then," said the boy. "Tell me a story."

68
The Sweetest Music

The youngest Muse, Calliope, had a son called Orpheus who played the sweetest music on earth. Wild beasts lay down and purred when they heard him play, and even the trees tore their roots out of the earth and followed after him when they heard his songs. Orpheus was in love with a girl called Eurydice, and on their wedding day his happy music made even the stars dance in the sky. But that night, as they were going home from the wedding party, Eurydice tripped and stepped on a poisonous snake which bit her in the heel. She fell down and died immediately, and Hermes whisked her spirit down to the Underworld.

Orpheus wept and wept so much that he almost lost his beautiful voice. He could not live without his Eurydice, so he decided to go down to Tartarus and get his bride back. Bravely he entered the dark entrance to Hades' kingdom, and as hope came back to him, he began to sing again.

The Underworld had never heard such music. The shimmering notes of the lyre sped downwards, and unlocked the barriers of death. Even the fierce three-headed dog Cerberus lay down and listened to Orpheus' song of love and loss.

Tartarus was still and silent. The souls of the dead no longer fluttered and whispered. Charon the old ferryman stilled his oars. Hades himself wept tears of pity as he heard Orpheus play.

"You may have your Eurydice back," he boomed. "But there is one condition. If you look back even once to see if she is following you up to earth, she will have to stay here forever. Only when you are both safely in the land of the living may you turn around." Orpheus agreed at once, and he and Eurydice swiftly set out for the earth above. The journey seemed to take a long time, and Orpheus was not at all sure that Eurydice was behind him. As he reached the light of day, he couldn't bear it a moment longer and he turned around. Eurydice had not quite reached the entrance. Orpheus shrieked with grief as Hermes dragged her down once again into the Underworld—this time forever. He ran weeping through the woods, playing a terrible sad lament, until he ran into a group of the mad Maenads.

"Join our dance," they cried, but Orpheus was crying so much that he didn't hear them, and so they tore him apart in a rage, and flung him into the river. In after times it was said that his head and his lyre floated on, still singing and playing, until they landed on the island of Lesbos and were taken up to the heavens and honoured among the stars. The Muses gathered up his torn body and buried it in a grove, and there the nightingales still sing more sweetly than anywhere else in the world. After the funeral, Orpheus's soul raced down to Tartarus, where he joined his beloved Eurydice forever.

Atticus hobbled along on a stick. "We shan't get to Troy at all at this rate," he grumbled, looking at his swollen toe. "I wish I could get this thorn out. I shall have to ask for a healer in the next village."

The healer tied the linen bandage off neatly. "It shouldn't give you any more trouble now," she said. Atticus fumbled in his wallet to pay her, but she shook her head. "You're a storyteller. You can pay me with a story while you rest that foot a bit."

69

The Centaur Healer

The goatherd called and whistled to his dog, but she took no notice, so he went to find her. She was lying on the ground together with his best nanny goat, and between their front legs was a baby boy, whom they were licking tenderly. The goatherd stooped to pick the boy up, but suddenly a bright light shone round him. The goatherd scratched his head. "Must be the child of a god," he thought. "Better leave it alone."

Later that day the baby, whose name was Asclepius, snuggled sleepily into his father Apollo's cloak, as he flew towards the centaur Chiron's cave on Mount Pelion. Chiron was the greatest teacher and healer of all time, and kings and princes were sent to him to learn how to be heroes.

Asclepius became Chiron's star pupil. He was eager to learn everything his master could teach, and soon he knew the use of every healing herb on earth as well as the meaning of every star in the sky. And what he didn't learn from Chiron, he learnt from his father, Apollo, who visited him often. When he grew up, he went to his master and knelt before him.

"Dear Chiron," he said. "I need to go out into the world. I want to help the people of Greece, and I want to teach others to heal." Chiron patted his head and gave him his blessing.

Asclepius soon had queues of sick people outside his little house. People on stretchers, people on crutches, people with cuts and fevers—everyone who came was treated, and they all left dancing and singing the praises of Asclepius the great doctor.

They liked him so much that they built temples in his honour, and Asclepius put beds in them, so that people could stay there and recover from their illnesses.

Asclepius had a tall staff, all twined round with living snakes, and as he went round the beds, he listened to the snakes, who told him many secrets about how to cure people. In time, he married, and he had seven children, all of whom he taught to be doctors too. His daughter, Hygeia, was very good at keeping people clean, and all her patients were scrubbed and healthy in no time at all.

Apollo was very proud of his son, and he persuaded the goddess Athene to give Asclepius two jars of the Gorgon Medusa's blood. The one from the right side of her body was used for bringing the dead back to life, and the one from the left could be used to kill. Asclepius never used the second, but he used the first one a great deal, and it was this that got him into trouble. Both the Fates and Hades complained to Zeus that their work was being interfered with, but Apollo showed Zeus how healthy everyone now was, and how much good his son was doing.

"I'll let him off this time," said Zeus. "But he mustn't use it again."

One day, Asclepius was approached by a man whose only son had died. "Please, please, please help him," wailed the man. "He's only seven! I'll give you anything!"

Now Asclepius felt so sorry for the man that he brought the boy back to life with the forbidden Gorgon's blood. The man was so grateful he gave Asclepius bags and bags of gold. But when Zeus found out he was furious, and he threw a thunderbolt which killed not only the man and his son, but Asclepius too.

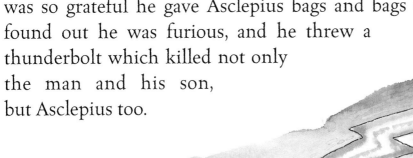

When Apollo saw the grey ashes that had been his son blowing about in the breeze, he was determined to have his revenge on Zeus. But Zeus was sorry for what he had done, and brought Asclepius back to life, later setting him and his serpents among the stars to shine his healing wisdom down on all doctors everywhere.

The wedding party danced up the road by the river, throwing flowers and garlands in front of the bride and groom.

"That reminds me of another wedding," said Atticus to Melissa as they passed. "Let's sit down and let them go by while I tell you the story."

70

The Goddesses' Quarrel

Prince Peleus was one of the pupils of Chiron the centaur. He was a great hunter and athlete, and a great favourite of the gods, too. "I think he deserves a nice wife," said Zeus to Hera one day, and Hera agreed.

"Perhaps he'd like Thetis the nymph, although I'm not sure she wants to marry a mortal," said Hera.

"Well, if he can catch her, he can have her," answered Zeus, and he flew straight down to Chiron's cave to give Peleus the good news. Peleus set out for the sea shore at once, and rowed himself to the tiny island where Thetis had gone to bathe, riding on the back of her pet dolphin. She was just taking a little nap on a bed of seaweed when Peleus grabbed her. She was so startled that she changed into a candle-flame, a jug of water, a lion and a snake, one after the other. Then she turned into a horrid slimy cuttlefish and squirted oily black ink at her husband to be, covering him from head to toe.

But Peleus never let go once, and when Thetis had calmed down, she agreed to marry him.

Hera sent her messenger Iris to everyone she could think of, inviting them all to the wedding outside Chiron's cave. When the day came, the gods and goddesses sat on silver thrones, Hera herself lit the wedding fire, and Zeus gave the bride away.

The Muses sang, and the nereids danced, and the endless stream of wonderful presents was displayed on the white white sand. There was a magic spear, and a golden suit of armour, a pair of immortal horses, and a magnificent chariot, as well as many other useful things for the young couple.

But Hera had forgotten to invite one person to the wedding. Eris, the spirit of strife, crouched behind a bush, muttering and moaning to herself as she watched the festivities.

"I'll teach them to be happy," she snarled, as she rolled one of her golden apples towards Peleus, who was talking to Hera, Aphrodite and Athene. As he noticed it, he picked it up, and read the writing on it out loud.

"*To the Fairest*," he said, puzzled. "Now who can this be for?" Hera, Aphrodite and Athene all rushed at him.

"It's mine!" shouted Hera, grabbing at it.

"No, mine!" yelled Aphrodite, pushing her away.

"Get off, it's mine!" screamed Athene, stepping on Aphrodite's toes. The three goddesses quarrelled so much that the whole wedding was spoiled, and they flew back to

Olympus, where they argued about who should have it for three whole months. Eris was delighted.

"If one little apple can do that, just think what a whole treeful could do!" she said to herself, chuckling evilly. And off she went to plant some special quick-growing apple seeds in her gloomy garden.

Atticus had met the shepherdess just as he and Melissa had got to the bottom of Mount Pelion.

"That's Chiron's cave," she told him, as they scrambled up together beside a tumbling stream. "You can still see some writing in there."

"I'm puffed out," said Atticus, when he'd had a look. "Why don't we sit on this big stone while I tell you a story? What would you like?"

"A story about Achilles," she said. "He's my favourite hero."

71
The Boy in the Fire

 King Peleus and Thetis the nymph had seven fine sons together, but Thetis was not happy.

"I never really wanted to marry a mortal," she grumbled as each child was born. "It's not fair that my children can't live forever like me." And so when each child was three days old, she hung him over a sacred fire and tried to burn away his mortal parts, afterwards rubbing him with ambrosia so that he could go and live on Olympus with the gods. Peleus was very sad at losing his sons like this, so when the seventh child was born, he determined that this one should stay on earth with him. As Thetis turned the boy this way and that over the sacred fire, holding him up by one heel, Peleus rushed in and snatched him.

"How dare you," cried Thetis, slapping him hard, and she was so angry that she rushed out of the palace and returned to the sea where she had been born, and never came back to her husband. Peleus took the crying baby and soothed him. He was now immortal, all except for the ankle and the back of the heel where his mother had been holding him. This bit was all burnt and red looking, so Peleus made his son a brand-new ankle and heel from the bones of a giant.

Peleus named his seventh son Achilles, and when he was old enough, he sent him away to be trained by Chiron the wise centaur, as Peleus had been himself. Achilles went on to be the greatest hero ever born—but in the end his mortal heel was the cause of his death in the great war of Troy.

Atticus and Melissa had walked into the bustling city of Iolcus that morning.

"Troy's getting closer!" he thought excitedly. Wagonloads of vegetables and grain blocked the narrow streets, and they had to fight their way through to the harbour. Suddenly Atticus heard someone shouting his name. It was Captain Nikos. Atticus was thankful to see him. Getting a ship from Iolcus wasn't easy, he'd heard.

"Do you think you could help me find a ship to Troy?" he asked hopefully.

"Nothing easier," said Nikos. "I'm going there myself tomorrow. You and Melissa can come with us. Come and meet the crew and tell us a story."

72
The Ship of Heroes

 King Pelias of Iolcus had a nephew called Jason, a strong, handsome young man who had been hidden in Chiron's cave since he was a child to keep him safe from his enemies. He was the true heir to the throne of Iolcus, and one day he decided to go and take his kingdom back from his wicked uncle. As he walked down the slopes of the mountain, he came to a river, where an old woman stood looking feebly at the foaming waters.

"Can I help you across, my lady?" he said politely. The old woman jumped on to his back without a word, and they set off. As Jason got further and further into the middle of the river, the old woman seemed to get heavier and heavier, until he was sinking into the mud at every step. As he struggled to reach the other side the sticky mud sucked one of his sandals off, and it was lost forever. Jason set the old lady down on the bank, and as he did so he gasped. There in front of his eyes was the goddess Hera, revealed in all her glory.

"You are a good boy to carry such a heavy load without complaining," she said. "I shall certainly help you to get your throne back." And she disappeared.

Jason limped into the palace, one sandal on and one sandal off. His Uncle Pelias noticed him at once and turned pale with horror. An oracle had

once told him that a boy with one sandal would overthrow him, so he knew just who Jason was.

However, he smiled sweetly and embraced his nephew, shouting orders for a great feast to be prepared. "Now, dear boy," he said. "You must certainly have your throne back, for I have reigned long enough. But first you must do a heroic deed to prove that you can be a good king to our people." Then he told Jason that he must go and fetch the magical golden fleece from the land of Colchis.

"When the fleece hangs in the throne room of Iolcus, then the crown will be yours," he said. What Pelias didn't say was that the fleece was guarded by a fierce dragon which never slept.

Jason gathered together all his old school friends, and together they built a wonderful ship which they called the *Argo*, with seeing eyes in the prow and fifty oars.

Before they set off they gave sacrifices to all the gods and goddesses, making sure that no one was left out or offended, and when the *Argo* sailed, she was full of fifty heroes, all ready for any kind of adventure. Heracles was there, with his friends Admetus and Hylas. Atalanta the huntress came, and so did Orpheus the poet and Castor and Polydeuces, the sons of Leda and Zeus. They called themselves the Argonauts, and Jason was their leader and captain.

The Argonauts sailed east, on and on, until they landed in a strange country to ask the way. All the people there were smiling and contented, except for the king, who was so thin and bony that he looked as if he might fall apart at any moment.

"Whatever is the matter?" asked Jason. The king explained that every night and morning he tried to eat, but as soon as the food was set on the table three revolting fat bird-women flew down and ate what was on his plate.

"They call themselves Harpies, and whatever they don't eat they sit in and make a mess of, so that it can't be touched," he whispered weakly. "None of my people can get rid of them, and believe me, we've tried!"

Jason and the Argonauts were hungry themselves, so they told the king to lay on a feast for that night.

As soon as the disgusting Harpies swooped into the room, Calaïs and Zetes, the sons of the North Wind, flew into the air with swords and sticks and chased and whipped the Harpies until they screamed and begged for their lives. The Argonauts laughed and cheered as they sat down to their dinner, and the king laughed with them as he stuffed food into his poor starved stomach. The Harpies never came back, and the Argonauts got back into *Argo* and sailed on towards Colchis.

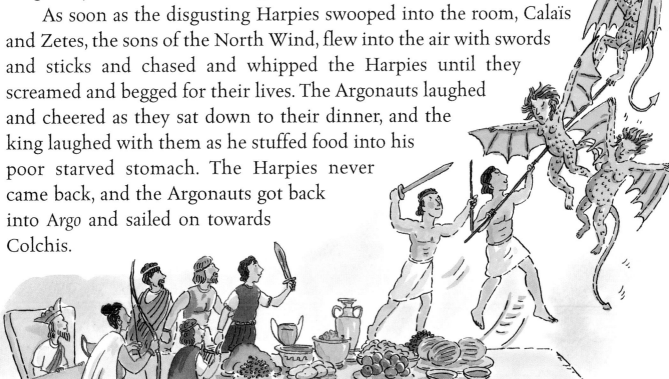

The king had warned them about the dangerous clashing rocks they would come to on the way, and told them how to avoid them.

"If you can row as fast as a racing pigeon can fly, then you will get through," he said. "Send a bird flying ahead of your ship and you will see."

The magic rocks ground and crashed together as the Argonauts rowed near, and they were all very frightened. Jason sent his pigeon on ahead at once, and it flew through the rocks like an arrow, coming out safe on the other side.

"Now row! Row for your lives," cried Jason, and Orpheus played a tune that made them pull with the strength of twenty men at each oar, while the goddess Hera pushed from behind. The *Argo* whizzed past the rocks with nothing to spare, and then they were through. The rocks settled into a calm sea, and never moved again. The Argonauts had broken their spell forever.

Although Hera helped Jason and his friends as much as she dared, there were many many more exciting adventures on their journey before they arrived safely in the city of Colchis, and set out to look for the golden fleece at last.

As Atticus stopped, the sailors all groaned. "You can't leave it there!" they said.

"Come on, boys!" said Captain Nikos. "There's work to be done. Let's load the ship, and then when we've finished, Atticus will tell us how Jason got the golden fleece. If you all work like those heroes on Argo it shouldn't take long."

Melissa trotted up the gangplank to her usual place, and soon everything was stowed. One by one the sailors sneaked up to Atticus and sat down. When Captain Nikos came aboard, he laughed.

"One more story for luck," he said. "Then I expect those sails ready in double quick time! We're catching the early tide."

73

The Impossible Task

The King of Colchis hated strangers. He hated them so much that he killed any who came to his country. But when he heard that Jason and his band of Argonauts had landed on his shores in search of the precious golden fleece, he smiled nastily.

"I shall set this great hero an impossible task, and *then* I shall kill him and his followers," he said to his witch-daughter Medea. So the king welcomed Jason and his friends, but when they told him what they had come for he pretended to be surprised.

"Don't you know that anyone who wants the golden fleece must do something for me first? I have a field that needs ploughing up and sowing— perhaps you could do that?" Jason agreed, but he was very surprised when he saw the king's plough animals, and even more surprised when he saw what he had to sow. The plough was harnessed to two fiery bulls, whose breath burned anyone who came near them, and the seeds in the packet were dragon's teeth.

"You have till sunset tomorrow," said the king.

Now Hera knew that Jason could never plough and sow the field on his own, so she summoned Aphrodite.

"Make the king's daughter, Medea, fall in love with Jason," she commanded. "She will know how to help him." So Aphrodite sent her son Eros to shoot Medea with his little love darts, and soon afterwards Medea sneaked into Jason's room.

"I love you," she whispered, "and I can help you. Take this lotion and cover yourself with it. Then you will be able to bear the heat of the bulls' breath and plough the field." Jason did just as she said, and then he sowed the dragon's teeth. Straightaway hundreds of stone soldiers sprang up in neat rows from the ground, but Jason threw a rock at them, and they all began to fight each other. By sunset they were all dead.

The king was furious, and he ordered his soldiers to kill Jason and his Argonauts at dawn. But Medea overheard his plan and ran to Jason at once.

"You must leave," she said. "I will lead you to the sacred grove, and sing the dragon to sleep with my magic while you steal the golden fleece. Then we can escape together." Jason kissed her, and together they tiptoed out of the palace.

The grove was dark and gloomy, but the golden fleece shone out like a thousand suns. Quickly Medea began to chant a magic song, and the green scaly dragon which had been set to guard the fleece closed its huge eyes with a sigh.

Jason stepped over its gigantic body and ripped the precious fleece from the branch where it hung. A hundred warning bells rang out as Jason and Medea ran for the *Argo* and they heard the thunder of many feet behind them as the king's soldiers gave chase. They flung themselves onto the deck, and the Argonauts rowed and rowed and rowed until Colchis was left far behind. The golden fleece was rescued at last, and Jason could now go home to Iolcus and claim his throne from his wicked uncle Pelias.

The ship slipped out of harbour in the early morning mist. The crew were all busy with the sails, so Atticus went to sit by Melissa.

"Last leg of the voyage, Melissa," he said. "Just think! All these months of travelling and we shall soon be in sight of Troy. It's a shame we don't have time to go through Thrace, and it's a pity we can't see the red anemones in flower on the mountains—but I'll tell you the story of how they got there. That'll have to do instead."

◉ 74 ◉

The Boy Whom Love Forgot

The myrrh tree stood waving and sighing in the breeze, the two halves of its trunk split down the middle. At its roots lay a beautiful newborn baby, gurgling and cooing as he waved his tiny fists in the air.

"What shall I do with you, my little Adonis?" said the goddess Aphrodite, as she stood looking down at him. "I'm sorry I turned your mother into a tree, but she really did annoy me. Ah well, I suppose I shall just have to look after you myself!" Now Aphrodite was really not very good at looking after babies, so she bundled Adonis into a nice cosy chest and took him down to Tartarus.

"There's a little secret of mine in here, Persephone," she said to the queen of the Underworld. "Keep it safe for me and I'll come back for it sometime." Persephone agreed, and she put the chest in a dark corner and completely forgot about it while she went up to the earth above to visit her mother, the goddess Demeter. But one day, soon after her return to Tartarus she was passing the chest and it gave a cry.

"Whatever is that?" said Persephone, and she opened the lid. What a surprise she got when she saw a lovely little boy smiling up at her. She lifted him out at once and took him to her own palace, where she petted him and spoiled him and gave him everything he wanted.

"How could Aphrodite leave you in a chest, my treasure?" she crooned. "Persephone will look after you now, my darling."

Now Aphrodite had forgotten all about Adonis, and she didn't remember until many years later when she saw Persephone again, smiling as she talked to a tall handsome youth.

"Who on earth is that gorgeous boy?" said Aphrodite, who had quite fallen in love with him. Persephone laughed.

"Why, that's your little secret that you left with me so many years ago!"

Aphrodite was furious. "How dare you steal him," she hissed, and soon the two goddesses were fighting as to who should have Adonis. The fight went on for so long that finally Zeus himself came down to settle it.

"The boy shall live four months with each of you, and have four months on his own," he boomed. But Aphrodite was determined to have Adonis all to herself. She put on her magic girdle and dazzled Adonis with her beauty, so that when it was Persephone's turn to have him, he wouldn't leave.

"The Underworld is so dark," he complained. "And you are so beautiful. Let me stay with you a little longer." Aphrodite smiled a secret smile as she agreed.

Persephone waited and waited for Adonis to come, and when he didn't arrive she went to look for him. She found him curled up asleep at Aphrodite's feet.

"Looking for someone?" asked Aphrodite sweetly. Persephone flounced out in a rage, and went straight to Ares, who agreed to help her to get her revenge.

As Adonis and Aphrodite were out hunting on Mount Lebanon the next day, a huge white boar charged out of the bushes and rushed at Adonis. Before Aphrodite could even scream a warning, Adonis had been gored to death by its sharp tusks. Wherever his blood fell on the earth, small red flowers appeared, and Aphrodite made them into garlands for her hair, so that she should always remember her beloved Adonis.

As they sat there the ship's mate, a rough-looking man with a villainous scar on his cheek, came rolling across the deck.

"Captain Nikos and the boys in the crew are asking if you'd tell us a story. The wind's set fair, and the ship'll sail herself for a while."

"I've got just the one," said Atticus, and soon the sailors were listening to the story of Paris and Oenone.

◩ 75 ◩
The Nymph and the Cowherd

The nymph Oenone sat on the edge of her fountain, spinning the pretty drops into a necklace as she sang to herself. It was no wonder that Paris the cowherd fell in love with her as soon as he saw her. When Oenone looked up and saw his handsome face staring at her from behind a tree she giggled shyly and dived back into the tinkling waters. But soon Paris had coaxed her out, and day after day they would sit together, holding hands and gazing into each other's eyes. Paris thought that Oenone was the most beautiful name in the world, and soon he had carved it onto the trunks of all the trees in the wood.

Paris was tall and strong and his eyes were as brown as new hazelnuts.

"I don't believe you're a cowherd at all," said Oenone. "I think you must be a king's son in disguise." And she was right, Paris was the son of Priam, the king of Troy. Agelaus, the king's chief herdsman, had been told to kill him when he was just a baby because of a prophecy that he would one day destroy his father's city. But Agelaus couldn't bring himself to do something so horrible, and so he had brought Paris up with his own son in secret.

When Paris grew up, he was put in charge of the king's best herd bulls, and his favourite game was to set them fighting with bulls from other herds.

"My bulls are always best," he boasted as he crowned the winner with flowers, and gave the loser an old straw hat to wear on his horns. Soon his bulls were winning all the time, and he decided to offer a golden crown to any bull which could beat the champion of them all.

Now the gods had been listening to Paris' boasting, and they decided to challenge him themselves. They came down and hid among the trees, and then sent Ares, disguised as a fierce black bull, to compete against Paris' champion. The fight went on for hours, but then Paris' bull began to tire.

"The golden crown is yours, oh great black bull," cried Paris at last. "You have beaten us fair and square." And all the gods came out to congratulate him on his decision. But Oenone sat weeping by her fountain, because she had seen in a dream that the gods would take Paris away from her, and that their happy life together in the woods would never be the same again.

"That Paris," said the ship's mate. "Wasn't he the one who caused all the trouble at Troy?" Atticus nodded.

"It was more than a bit of trouble," he said. "The Trojan War lasted for ten years, and all because the gods chose the wrong man to make an important decision. Listen, and I'll tell you the story."

◙ 76 ◙
The Fairest Goddess

After the wedding of King Peleus and Thetis the nymph, the gods and goddesses all went back to Olympus. But Olympus was no longer the happy place it had once been, because Hera, Athene and Aphrodite never stopped fighting and arguing over who should own the golden apple which was labelled 'To the Fairest'. They screeched and squawked and scratched like battling cats until everyone had to stick their fingers in their ears to shut out the horrible noise. Finally Zeus and the other gods decided that someone would have to judge between them. None of the gods dared to do it, so they chose a young cowherd, Paris, the son of King Priam of Troy. The gods liked Paris. He was good-looking and brave, and he seemed to be fair-minded and honest. So Zeus sent Hermes to fetch him to a meadow on Mount Ida, near Troy.

Paris couldn't help being a little nervous. The three goddesses were lined up in a row, each dressed in her best robes and her finest jewellery.

"They're all so beautiful," he whispered. "Maybe I should just divide the apple into three." But Hermes shook his head.

"Zeus himself has commanded you to make this choice," he said sternly. "And I really don't think you want to disobey him." Paris sighed unhappily and walked across the meadow, the golden apple in his hand.

"Now, dear goddesses," said Paris. "You each have five minutes to tell me why you are more beautiful than your friends. When you have all finished, then I shall decide between you."

Hera immediately stepped forward and took Paris by the arm.

"Dearest boy," she said. "Surely you can see that the prize should go to me. After all, Zeus himself did choose me over all the others. And besides, if you choose me, I shall make you the most powerful king in the world. Just imagine . . . palaces full of gold, countries to rule. Everyone would have to do as you ordered. Surely you can see that the apple belongs to me."

Paris scratched his head. He was very good at herding his bulls around, but he wasn't sure he wanted to be in charge of lots of countries. It sounded like too much hard work.

"Next, please," he said, as Hera went back to her place.

Then Athene walked across the grass, and clapped an arm around his shoulders. Paris nearly fell over.

"Only the most beautiful woman in the world could have armies falling at her feet," she said. "And if you choose me, you shall command them all. You shall be my best general, and I shall make you a famous hero. Give me the apple and you shall have the strength of twenty men and the courage of a hundred lions. No spear or sword shall ever wound you, and your shield shall turn any arrows back on those who fire them."

Paris rubbed his nose thoughtfully. Battles were noisy, and he didn't like blood much, although being that strong was quite tempting.

"Next, please," he called, as Athene strode back to her place in the line.

Only Aphrodite was left, and as she glided across the grass towards Paris she secretly slipped on her magic girdle.

"Dearest Paris," she purred. "Who else but the goddess of love could be the most beautiful woman ever?" Paris nodded dumbly as Aphrodite put her arm around his shoulders. She smelled deliciously of summer roses and dew. "You don't need kingdoms or armies, but what you do need is a bride almost as beautiful as me. If you give me the apple, I will let you marry Helen of Sparta, who is the loveliest mortal woman on earth." Now Aphrodite knew perfectly well that Helen was already happily married to King Menelaus of Sparta—in fact it was she who had made Helen fall in love with him—but she didn't care one little bit. She wanted that apple so badly that she would have done anything to get it.

Paris beamed at her. The most beautiful woman in the world—that sounded just what he wanted most. He forgot all about his love for the nymph Oenone, as he fell on his knees before Aphrodite.

"The apple is yours, oh fairest of all goddesses," he croaked. There was a whisk of cloaks and a stamp of feet as Hera and Athene stormed off in a jealous rage to plot and plan their revenge against him. But Aphrodite just smiled a secret smile of triumph as she raised Paris to his feet.

"Let's go and plan a wonderful wedding for you, my dear," she said.

The wind had got up, and the sails were flapping in a worrying way. Atticus huddled beside Melissa as sailors scurried about the ship.

"Looks like we're in for a summer storm," shouted Captain Nikos as he wrestled with the rudder. "Best stay down where you are."

Melissa's ears drooped miserably as the boat tossed. Atticus patted her.

"Don't worry, old girl, Nikos is a good sailor. He'll get us through this. I'll tell you a story to take your mind off the weather."

77

The Greeks' Bargain

Helen of Sparta had skin like a perfect peach and long dark hair that shone like a raven's wing. Her lips were the deep red of rosepetals and when she smiled the people around her would shade their eyes and look to see if the sun had come out.

Every prince in Greece was madly in love with her, and when she was old enough to be married, they all brought rich gifts to tempt her into choosing one of them as her husband. Tyndareus, her stepfather, would not let her accept any of the presents.

"We don't want them to think you have any favourites, my dear," he said wisely. In private, though, Tyndareus was worried. Every night he tossed and turned beside his wife, Leda, as he tried to think of a way to choose a husband for Helen without offending any of the other princes.

"It can't be done," he said despairingly. But the next morning Odysseus came to see him. Odysseus was the king of Ithaca and the son of

Sisyphus Sharp-Eyes, and he was very cunning. He knew he wasn't rich or powerful enough to marry Helen himself, and anyway, he was in love with a girl called Penelope. But Penelope's father didn't like him one bit.

"If I help you to find a way of finding a husband for Helen without offending anyone," he said, "will you help me to marry Penelope?" Tyndareus said yes at once. He knew how clever Odysseus was.

"This is what you have to do," said Odysseus. "Give Helen a golden wreath, and blindfold her. Then make the suitors all stand in a circle around her. Turn her around three times, and then make her walk towards them. Whoever she crowns first will be her husband."

"But the ones who have to go away will still be offended," said Tyndareus nervously.

"Ah!" laughed Odysseus. "But this is the clever part. Before Helen chooses you must make the suitors swear an unbreakable oath to support her choice and to defend her husband against anyone who takes her away from him. That way, no one can be upset or all the others will be against him."

Tyndareus agreed that this was a brilliant idea, and the very next day he carried out the plan. When the kings and princes had promised in front of the gods themselves to support Helen's future husband, Helen was blindfolded and given a golden wreath.

"Oh goddess of love, please let me crown Menelaus," she whispered under her breath, and Aphrodite heard her. Suddenly a tiny pinprick of light appeared before Helen's eyes. Aphrodite had made a secret hole in the blindfold.

"One!" shouted the men in the circle.

"Two!" as Helen was twirled and whirled around.

"Three!" as she staggered and nearly fell with dizziness. As she regained her balance, she walked straight towards the handsome prince of her dreams and put the wreath onto his head.

Menelaus and Helen were married at once, and after Tyndareus died, Menelaus became king of Sparta. After the wedding the kings and princes went back to their homes, but in their hearts each secretly hoped never to be called on to fulfil their great oath. Little did they know that the gods themselves had planned for them to have to.

Lightning flashed, and thunder crashed overhead. The sails were now lashed tight to the mast, and Captain Nikos and his crew were struggling to steer the ship away from the shore. Atticus spat out a mouthful of seawater as the wind roared and howled around the ship. He was kneeling with his arm around Melissa, who was lying on the deck, her eyes wide with fear. Atticus felt a tap on his back. It was the ship's boy.

"I'm so frightened, Atticus," he whimpered.

"Me too," said Atticus. "But these summer storms soon blow over. I'll tell you a story to pass the time."

◻ 78 ◻
The Face That Launched a Thousand Ships

Priam, king of Troy, opened his arms wide. "My dear son," he said, tears trickling down his cheeks. "Can you ever forgive me? Welcome home." And he gave Paris a big hug. Just then there was a commotion at a nearby window.

"Woe!" shrieked a girl's voice. "Woe to Troy! I see death and war and disaster!"

"Who on earth is that?" asked Paris nervously.

"Oh, that's just our sister Cassandra," said his brother Hector. "We never take any notice of her, she's always moaning on. Thinks she can see into the future or something."

Paris had arrived in Troy the day before. He had been determined to attend the great games held every year in honour of the son King Priam had sent off to be murdered by his chief herdsman. Priam had felt guilty about his dreadful deed ever since.

"I think it's time that murdered son came back to life," Paris said to his foster father Agelaus. But Agelaus had shaken his head. "You have your wonderful bulls, what more do you want?" he asked.

And when he had gone to Oenone's fountain to say goodbye, she had clung to him, crying. "If you are ever wounded, come back to me. I am the only one who can heal you," she sobbed as he strode off.

Paris had entered every event in the games, and won them all.

"Who is this magnificent young man?" whispered the crowd. "Surely he must be a prince."

As Paris came forward to collect his winner's crown from King Priam, Agelaus had stepped out of the crowd. "Your Majesty," he cried. "Forgive me! This is your long-lost son, returned from the dead. I didn't kill him after all." And Priam had wept with joy at the news.

"Better that Troy is destroyed than that I should lose my beloved son again," he said to the priests who reminded him of the old prophecy that Paris would one day bring disaster to the city.

Paris was popular with everyone, and soon his father was talking about finding him a wife. Paris just laughed. "Only the best in Greece will do for me," he said, remembering Aphrodite's promise to him.

A few nights later Aphrodite came to him in secret.

"King Menelaus is arriving in Troy tomorrow," she said. "Ask to go with him to Sparta, and then I will arrange for his wife Helen to fall in love with you. You can escape back to Troy with her, and then you will be married." Paris was very excited. He couldn't wait to see the famous Helen. He pretended to make friends with Menelaus at once, and begged him to let him visit Sparta.

"I have heard so much about your famous city, and I would love to come and see it," he lied. Menelaus agreed, and soon they had set sail. Priam had given Paris a beautiful ship with a figurehead of Aphrodite on the prow, and the goddess sent gentle breezes to help them on their way.

The palace at Sparta was huge and impressive with blood-red walls and heavy golden gates which opened with a blast of trumpets as Menelaus and Paris approached.

"Behold the king!" cried a herald as a tall woman came running out. She ran to Menelaus and flung her arms around him.

"I am so glad you're back, dear husband," she said. "I have missed you so much." Paris's mouth fell open at his first sight of Helen. She was definitely the most beautiful woman he had ever seen, although he didn't think he would tell Aphrodite that.

That night, after a wonderful welcome feast, Aphrodite made her son Eros invisible and sent him to shoot one of his love darts into Helen's heart. Although she had loved Menelaus ever since she could remember, the minute the dart touched Helen's skin she could think of nothing and nobody but Paris.

"Dear prince," she whispered, as she passed him in the corridor. "Take me away from this horrible place. I can't think why I ever married that stupid Menelaus!" So later that night Paris knocked at Helen's door, and disguised in thick black cloaks, they galloped through the night, sneaked aboard his ship and set sail.

"I will never let you go," he vowed as he kissed her. "Not if all the kings of Greece come knocking at the gates of Troy."

When Menelaus discovered where Helen had gone, he was furious.

"I'll teach that Trojan rogue to steal my wife!" he roared, stomping round the throne room in a rage. "Send messengers to all the kings and princes. It is time for them to keep the promises they made when I married her. I shall launch a thousand ships to get her back! We will go to war!" And he went off to order his army and his fleet to make ready.

Slosh, slurp, squelch, slosh, slurp, squelch *went the buckets as everyone helped to bail out the ship. The storm had blown them off course, and they were sheltering in a little bay off the island of Euboea.*

"We'll go ashore after this and sacrifice to the gods for keeping us safe," said Captain Nikos. The sailors all nodded.

"Doesn't do to offend the gods," they said.

After they had made their sacrifice of wine and salt, the sailors sat down to eat their soggy bread and olives.

"How about a story, Atticus?" said Nikos.

"I'll tell you how the Greek fleet got stuck in Aulis, just over there," said Atticus, pointing west over the hills.

79
The Sacrifice of a Princess

Menelaus's Greek fleet of a thousand ships had just gathered near Aulis for the second time. Many delays and false starts had prevented them from setting off before. Odysseus was there, with his men of Ithaca, so was Achilles with his best friend Patroclus and their soldiers, together with many other kings, princes and heroes. The captains of the fleet were King Agamemnon, Menelaus's brother, and King Idomeneus of Crete.

"Let us start at once, my brothers!" cried Agamemnon from the deck of his great fighting galley. "Forward to Troy!" There was a huge cheer as the sails were raised, and the mass of ships moved forward. But as they reached the mouth of the harbour a strong wind rose up from the north-east and drove them back. It blew and blew and blew for days and days, until Agamemnon thought they would never be able to leave. He called for his soothsayer, Calchas.

"Tell us what to do, old man," he commanded. So Calchas cast his magic stones and muttered and mumbled as he looked for an answer from the gods. Finally he looked up.

"You have offended the goddess Artemis," he said in his wheezy voice. "You must sacrifice the prettiest of your daughters to her, or you will never get away."

Agamemnon was horrified. "Sacrifice my daughter, Iphigenia?" he cried. "What will my wife Clytemnestra say?"

But when the Greek kings heard the news, they insisted that Iphigenia be sent for.

"We won't go to war with you if you don't," they said. So poor Iphigenia was brought to Aulis to be sacrificed. She was very frightened, but very brave, and as she stood on the altar in her simple white dress, Agamemnon wept as he watched and had to be dragged away.

"I am doing this freely, for my father, for the goddess and for Greece," Iphigenia said as she bared her graceful neck for the axe. Now Artemis loved brave people, and so she flew down at once in a cloud of silver raindrops and seized Iphigenia away to safety just as the axe fell. At that minute, the wind dropped and began to blow in the right direction. The kings and their men whooped as they ran back to the ships and set sail immediately.

"Trojans beware!" bellowed King Agamemnon joyfully as he jumped aboard. "The Greeks are coming to get you!"

The sky was washed clean of clouds and the sun shone brightly over the ship as its sails filled with the brisk southwesterly wind. "Perfect!" shouted Captain Nikos. "We shall be at Troy in no time with this breeze!"

Atticus leant over the side, watching the clear blue water slip by.

"Did I ever tell you how Odysseus nearly didn't go to Troy?" he asked Melissa.

⧉ 80 ⧉
The King Who Ploughed Sand

King Menelaus and his herald, the hero Palamedes, rode the length and breadth of Greece calling up the kings and princes to war.

Tantara tantara tantara called the great brass trumpet, as Menelaus landed on the island of Ithaca, and set off towards Odysseus's palace.

Now Odysseus was as cunning as a thousand weasels and as slippery as a bucketful of eels. He didn't want to keep his promise to Menelaus and go to war at all, because Zeus's oracle had once told him that if he did, the gods wouldn't let him return for twenty years, and that when he did come back he would be a beggar. Odysseus didn't want to leave his comfortable palace and his full wine cellar, and he certainly didn't want to spend twenty years away from his beautiful wife, Penelope, and his little son Telemachus.

"You must lie for me," he hissed at Penelope as he ran out of the back door. "Tell them I've gone mad and am doing something strange on the beach and can't come." He went quickly to a shepherd's hut and changed into some dirty ragged old clothes and a stupid-looking pink felt hat shaped like half an egg. Then he led a great big ox and a tiny little donkey down to the field at the edge of the beach and harnessed them to an old plough.

Menelaus and Palamedes were very angry when they heard why Odysseus was not at home.

"Mad?" roared Menelaus. "He's no more mad than I am! Take us to him at once." So Penelope bundled Telemachus into a sling and led them down to the beach.

As they got nearer they heard a strange song being sung in a high, cracked voice.

Plant the seaweed,
Make it grow,
Plough the sand
When tides are low . . .

And there was Odysseus skipping and singing up and down the beach throwing handsful of salt over his shoulder as he tried to plough a straight furrow with the ox and the donkey. He wasn't doing a very good job of it. When Odysseus saw Penelope, Menelaus and Palamedes approaching he stopped and leaned on the plough handle.

"Ooh! Fine strangers to see poor little Odysseus plant his seaweed!" he giggled, rolling his eyes madly. "And who might you be, lovely lady?"

Menelaus stamped his foot.

"Stop this silliness at once and come and keep your promise to me!" he growled. But Odysseus just danced a little jig and carried on ploughing.

"Right!" said Palamedes. "I've had enough of this. Let's see if he really is mad and doesn't recognise us." He snatched Telemachus out of Penelope's arms and laid him down in the path of the plough. On and on came the stamping hooves, but just at the last minute Odysseus pulled on the reins and stopped them. He ran to pick up his son.

"All right, Palamedes," he said. "I accept my fate. You win." And he went to order his soldiers and his warships to make ready.

So Odysseus and his fleet went to join the other Greek kings at Aulis. He kissed Penelope and Telemachus with tears running down his cheeks.

"Never forget me," he begged. "And however long it takes for me to return, you will wait for me, won't you?" Penelope promised that she would— but she never guessed how hard it would be for her to keep that promise in the long empty years to come.

They landed on Lemnos two days later. Captain Nikos decided to spend a few days on the island repairing the rudder, which had been damaged in the storm.

"Can't sail up the Hellespont with no rudder," he said grimly. "Too dangerous." Melissa wobbled off the boat thankfully—a donkey's legs are not meant for sea journeys, and she wanted grass. She and Atticus wandered off to explore.

"You know, Melissa," said Atticus. "If it hadn't been for a man who lived on Lemnos, the Greeks could never have won the Trojan War." Melissa snorted. She was more interested in eating than stories at the moment, but she flicked back her ears to listen as Atticus began his tale.

◙ 81 ◙
The Smelly Wound

When Heracles had died and gone up to Olympus to live with the gods, he had given his great bow and arrows to the man who had lit his funeral pyre, a young man called Philoctetes. Philoctetes was almost as strong as Heracles himself, so although no other man on earth could use the bow, Philoctetes had no trouble in drawing the string back to his shoulder.

"It's as easy as eating cherries," he boasted, and when Menelaus's call to war went out, Philoctetes was one of the first to join up.

"You'll need me before this is all over, I expect," he said. "After all I am the greatest archer in all of Greece." So as the Greek fleet set sail at last, Philoctetes and his bow went with them. Soon they came to a little island, where they stopped to take on water. "Just going to stretch my legs," said Philoctetes, leaping out onto the shore. But he didn't look before he jumped down, and he landed on a horrible poisonous snake, which bit him on the foot.

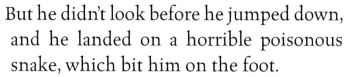

"Aaargh!" he screamed, thrashing and crashing around with the pain. His friends soon came running, and they cut a cross in between the fang marks and sucked out the poison. But they didn't suck out all of it, and soon Philoctetes' foot was swollen to the size of a football. The ships sailed on towards Troy, but as they got nearer and nearer, Philoctetes' wound began to get smellier and smellier. Soon everyone in the fleet was holding their noses against the terrible stench.

Just outside the entrance to the Hellespont lies the island of Lemnos, and it was there that the kings and captains decided to leave poor Philoctetes all by himself to get better.

"We really can't have him with us," they whispered. "He just smells too disgusting." So at dead of night they lifted Philoctetes into a little boat, together with some food and water and his precious bow and arrows and rowed him out to the island, where they dumped him on the beach. By this time he was feeling too ill to care about anything, but in about a week the wound began to crust over, and although it still smelled disgusting, Philoctetes could hobble about enough to catch food and find water. He was very cross at being left behind, but there was nothing he could do. He never guessed that it would be nearly ten years before he saw his friends again, and that his wound would still be as smelly as ever when he did. But that is quite another story.

They had just landed at the harbour near Troy and Atticus had butterflies in his stomach. He and Melissa got off the ship and walked into a jostling mass of people.

"This way for the storytelling festival!" a man was shouting. Captain Nikos was busy supervising the unloading of his cargo, but he had promised Atticus that he and the crew would come and see him perform.

Now Atticus had to register for the competition. There was a long queue.

"We'll just have to wait," he muttered to Melissa. "I'll tell you a story very quietly, to keep me calm."

82

The Cunning Plan

Although the Greek kings had many men, horses and weapons, they hadn't been able to bring enough provisions for a whole army. So before they attacked the city of Troy itself, they first had to conquer all the cities and towns and farmland around it so that they could feed themselves. It took them nine long years of fighting and effort, and at the end of it even the heroes among them were weary and longing for home. But at last they reached the Great Plain of Troy and set up camp. Then from the tops of their crowded ramparts the people of Troy could see huge amounts of stores and horses and armour hidden behind the high wall that the Greeks had built to protect their ships from the Trojan army. A thousand tents and a thousand banners flapped in the breeze, and the smoke of a thousand campfires swirled and whirled in the air, bringing wafts of cooking meat and simmering beans to the worried citizens.

"We are doomed," wailed Cassandra, King Priam's daughter. "Doomed!" But as usual no one took any notice of her.

King Priam and his counsellors were in the throne room, having a meeting.

"We must send for our ally King Rhesus at once," said King Priam. "The priests have just reminded me of a prophecy. It says that once his white horses have drunk from the River Scamander, Troy will stand for ever and ever. No one will be able to beat us." So a messenger was sent, and soon the news came that King Rhesus, his horses and his army were on their way.

Now King Menelaus had just captured a Trojan spy called Dolon. Dolon was a terrible coward, so he had told Menelaus all about the prophecy.

"We must stop these horses drinking from the river," said Menelaus, and he sent for Odysseus and his friend Diomedes at once. "Think of a cunning plan," he begged them.

Cunning plans were what Odysseus was best at, and soon he had come up with a brilliant one.

He and Diomedes sneaked past the enemy sentries at dead of night and killed King Rhesus as he slept in his tent. Then they stole his beautiful white horses. Tiptoeing out of the enemy camp, they put them onto a ship and sent it far, far away. The horses never drank a drop from the River Scamander, and as their master was dead, the prophecy never came true.

"I really am the most cunning man in the world," said Odysseus gleefully as he and Diomedes celebrated their success. However, the Greeks would need a lot more than cunning to win the war and return Helen to her husband.

By the time Atticus had settled Melissa and found a corner to sleep in he was tired.

"Two hundred competitors so far, and more coming in all the time," he yawned. "How will they manage to hear all of us?"

The next morning he and Melissa walked towards the walls of Troy with Callimachus, a boy who had slept beside them the night before. Callimachus had travelled all the way from Cyrene in Libya to come to the Festival, and he had been begging Atticus to tell him a story ever since they woke up.

" 'Good fortune will come from Cyrene's son,' "Atticus remembered. "I wonder if the oracle at Delphi meant that this boy is going to bring me luck?"

83
The Hero Who Sulked

The Greeks shivered and shook and groaned behind their high wall. The war had not been going at all well, and now they had all been struck down by a terrible plague, which gave them boils in nasty places and hot horrible headaches which felt as if monsters were trampling their skulls. It was all King Agamemnon's fault. He had stolen a beautiful girl named Chryseis from her father, a priest of Apollo, and made her into his slave. This had annoyed the god, and so he had begun to shoot his dreadful Plague Arrows into the Greek camp.

"That will soon make Agamemnon give her back," Apollo said to Chryseis's father, who had come to him for help.

Now Chryseis had a friend called Briseis who had been captured at the same time. Agamemnon had given Briseis to Achilles as a present, but when he found that the only way to stop the plague was to give Chryseis back to her father, he went to Achilles' tent and took his gift back.

"Sorry, old chap," he said. "But you don't really need her, do you?" This made Achilles so angry that he stomped into his tent and refused to come out, even when the fighting got really fierce and the Trojans started winning.

"I shan't put on even one piece of armour till Agamemnon apologises," he muttered to his best friend Patroclus. Patroclus loyally stayed with Achilles in the hot stuffy tent all that day and night, but finally, as dawn broke, and he heard the clash of swords and spears begin the battle again, he couldn't bear it any longer.

"Look, Achilles," he said, "the Trojans are trying to burn Ajax's ships, and—oh no! Diomedes and Odysseus are both wounded. We must go and help them!"

Achilles just turned his back. "Serves them right!" he mumbled. But as the day went on, he began to feel guilty, as more and more of his friends were wounded or killed. Patroclus finally persuaded Achilles to lend him his golden armour and helmet, and to let him lead Achilles' troops out to help the Greeks.

"The Trojans will think it's you," he said. "It'll be funny to see how fast they run away!"

As Patroclus and his men charged towards them, the Trojans began to panic.

"Oh no! It's Achilles the Awful!" they cried, as they flung down their weapons. Only their leader, Prince Hector, stood firm. When Patroclus came

near him, followed by the whole Greek army, he raised his spear and flung it at Hector. But the spear clanged on Hector's shield and fell uselessly to the ground.

As Achilles stood outside his tent and watched, Hector's own great spear sailed through the air and hit Patroclus with a deadly blow. Patroclus fell to the ground, and Achilles knew that his best friend in the whole world was dead. He began to tear his hair and wail.

"Oh why why why did I let him go?" he screamed, and then he shook his fist at the Trojans, who were retreating, carrying the golden armour that Patroclus had borrowed.

That night, Achilles asked his mother Thetis to get him some new armour, and by morning the god Hephaestus had forged him a suit like nothing that has ever been made before or since. It was all of gold and silver, with pictures of gods and battles so cunningly hammered into the metal that the figures looked quite alive.

"I hope you're ready for me, Hector," said Achilles grimly, as he went to sharpen his sword and spear for the battle ahead. "Because I'm coming to kill you."

Atticus was surprised at how small old Troy actually was. Although there were now new houses and hovels scattered higgledy-piggledy around it, the citadel itself was tiny. Atticus stood under the Great Gate, holding Melissa's rope, and looked admiringly at the thick walls.

"I understand now how Achilles was able to chase Hector three times round the city boundary," he said to Callimachus. "I always wondered about that."

"Tell me the story," said Callimachus eagerly.

84

Revenge!

Before he went out to fight against Hector, Achilles made peace with Agamemnon. The great king came out of his tent, wild-haired and red-eyed from weeping all night for the many heroes who had died or been wounded in battle the day before. He held out his arms and Achilles embraced him silently. Then Agamemnon gave the slave-girl Briseis back to Achilles, together with gifts of gold and jewels.

"Friends should not fight," he said hoarsely. "Will you forgive me?" And then Achilles wept too, great silver tears that ran down his armour like a bright river. Just then the sun rose from behind the dark hills, and the battle trumpets began to sound.

"To war!" cried Achilles, leaping into his chariot and thundering off across the plain with all that was left of the Greek army running and yelling behind. It was a terrifying sight, but Hector of Troy was a brave man. All his troops had fled once more at the sight of Achilles, so he stood alone in front of the Great Gate of Troy. As Achilles came nearer and nearer he raised the golden spear that had killed Patroclus, and began to charge. As he ran, he flung the spear as hard as he could, but Achilles' new shield had so much magic in it that the spear bounced off harmlessly. Then Hector drew his sword and tried to leap into the chariot beside Achilles. But Achilles leapt out of the chariot, and started to chase him round the city walls. Three times round they went, slashing and stabbing at each other, until at last the two heroes were so out of breath that they stopped once more before the Great Gate of Troy. Then Achilles raised his spear high above his head, and as he lunged forward and stabbed Hector in the chest he cried out.

"Hear me, my Patroclus! Your death is avenged!" Hector sank down dying to the bare brown earth, and Achilles bent over him in triumph.

"I shall leave your wretched body here for the wolves and eagles to tear!" he hissed. But Hector opened both his eyes very wide and looked Achilles in the face.

"Let my father pay gold to get my body back, so that I can be buried in my beloved Troy," he gasped. "If you do not, then you will die here, before this very gate. Remember me when the arrow flies . . ." Then he fell back dead. Not a bird sang, not a sword rattled, not a speck of dust moved—all was as still and silent as if the gods themselves were listening.

A great scream of anger and grief went up from the high walls of Troy as Achilles tied the dead Hector's heels to his chariot, and dragged his body all round the battlefield, round and round and round and round. At last, as night fell, the Great Gate opened and an old man stepped out, dressed all in rags, with dust all over his grey head and beard. As he walked through the dusk towards the Greek camp, they saw that he was carrying a sign of peace.

"What do you want, old man," said Achilles roughly, as he approached the chariot, where Hector's body lay sprawled in the dirt.

"I am Priam, king of Troy," the old man whispered sadly. "I have come for my son's body, so that I can bury him as a prince deserves. Let me take him home."

But Achilles was still so angry with Hector for killing Patroclus, that he refused.

"The only way you will get him, Your Majesty, is to bring me his bodyweight in gold. Until then he shall lie here in the dust where he belongs."

Priam trudged wearily back to Troy and opened up his treasury. There was not much left in it. So he asked his people to help. Soon a heavy blanketful of gold was heaped on the ground beside Hector's body, which was now lying in a huge sling, on one side of an enormous pair of scales.

"Let's see if it's enough!" said Achilles. "Throw the gold onto the other side." Slowly, slowly Hector's body rose up, but as the last piece of gold was tipped in, the scales were not quite even. A groan went up from the Trojans, but just then a girl stepped forward. It was Polyxena, Hector's sister.

"Here, dearest brother," she said softly. "Take my rings and bracelets. I don't need them now." As Polyxena's jewellery fell with a clink onto the heap, the scales levelled.

"Enough!" roared Achilles. "Take the body!" But as the silent, solemn procession marched slowly back to Troy, his eyes could only see one thing—Polyxena's beautiful sad face. Achilles buried his face in his hands and wept as he realised that he had fallen in love with the sister of the man he had just killed.

It was several days till the competition started, so Atticus hobbled Melissa and left her to graze for the afternoon.

"I'm going down to the shore to get away from the crowds," he said to Callimachus, who reminded him of his son Geryon. "Want to come?"

"Will you tell me a story, then?" asked Callimachus.

"We—ell," Atticus said slowly. "It might stop me feeling so nervous, and they do say practice makes perfect." Callimachus whooped and leapt in the air.

85
The Hero's Heel

Achilles paced up and down his tent. *Stomp stomp stomp . . . turn . . . stomp stomp stomp . . .* turn. His mind was filled with pictures of Polyxena's beautiful face.

"How could she ever love her brother's murderer?" he muttered sadly to himself. Suddenly there was a flutter of wings, and a white dove flew through the doorway and landed on his shoulder. It had a message tied to its leg.

'*Meet me by the Great Gate at midnight*,' read Achilles eagerly. It was signed with a 'P'.

" 'P' for Polyxena," said Achilles. "Maybe she loves me after all."

The day passed as slowly as if it were made of thick dripping treacle. There was no fighting, because the Trojans were still in mourning

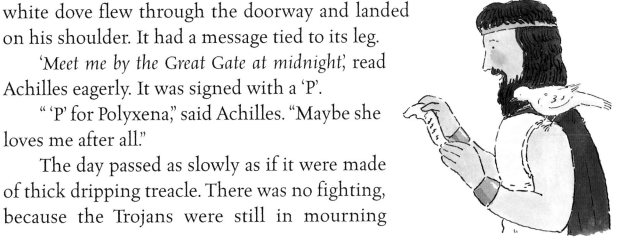

for their beloved Prince Hector. Achilles spent the long hours polishing his armour until it would have blinded the sun himself. He sharpened his weapons till they were like razors. As midnight approached, Achilles put on his best robes over his armour, and strapping a dagger to his side just in case, he sneaked out of the camp and across the plain. It was a still night, and the moon had not yet risen when he approached the Great Gate. A dark cloaked figure glided out from its shadow.

"Polyxena! My love!" gasped Achilles. But the figure did not speak. It just beckoned. His heart beating very fast, Achilles followed the figure through a little side door, and through the silent streets of Troy until it led him into the temple of the god Apollo. Candles were burning around the altar, and the place was heavy with the sweet smells of incense and oil. The figure threw back its hood, and in the dim light, Achilles saw the face of his beloved Polyxena.

"Let us pray to Apollo together," she whispered.

As Achilles knelt down on one knee, his mortal heel was bared. *Hiss! Thunk!* went an arrow, straight into his weak spot.

"Take that, murderer!" cried two voices, and as he looked up in agony, he saw Paris step out from behind a pillar to join his sister Polyxena.

"You!" cried Achilles. "Haven't you caused enough trouble already?" But Paris just laughed, and Polyxena with him. Wild, high, mad laughter it was, and Achilles had to get away from it. Stumbling and tripping, he limped back the way he had come, through the winding streets, out of the little door, until he was on the plain again. The pain in his heel was a burning fire now, and he knew that the arrow had been poisoned. Collapsing in front of the Great Gate of Troy, he remembered Hector's dying words with a shiver. Then, as he felt the last breath going out of him, he let out a great shriek.

"Mother!" he cried. "Mother, save me!" And Thetis heard him. Weeping with grief, she came out of the waves followed by her nereid maidens. But she was too late. As dawn broke she carried her dead son through the sobbing ranks of the Greek army and laid him on a funeral pyre. For seventeen days and nights the nine Muses chanted a solemn dirge over his ashes, while the Greeks held funeral games in his honour.

"He was the greatest hero of us all," they said. "He will never be forgotten as long as the tale of Troy is told." And he never has been.

As he finished, Atticus turned to look at Mount Ida to the south.

"So what happened then?" asked Callimachus.

"Well," said Atticus. "The Greeks were in trouble without their hero, Achilles, of course. They'd been in Troy for nearly ten years, and most of them wanted to go home. So Agamemnon asked Calchas the seer to cast an oracle to tell them how it would all turn out in the end."

86
The Arrows of Death

Calchas staggered out of his tent, plumes of smoke following him from the sacrificial fires. Agamemnon and the other kings watched him, anxious to hear what he had to say about their fates.

Troy cannot fall, nor Greeks go home,
Till he who's wounded to the bone
With serpent's tooth comes to this shore.
Then Trojan might shall fight no more.
But if he comes, he cannot win
Till hero's son comes riding in.
You need these two, plus arrows and bow
To save you all from strife and woe,
wheezed Calchas in his cracked old voice.

"But what does it all *mean*?" asked the kings anxiously. "Who *are* these men he's talking about?" Then Odysseus laughed.

"One of them is Philoctetes, of course. The one with the smelly wound who owns Heracles' bow and arrows! And the other must be Achilles' son Neoptolemus. Diomedes and I will go and get them." So off set Odysseus and Diomedes, and while Neoptolemus was delighted to join them, it took every last drop of Odysseus' trickery and cunning to persuade Philoctetes to come to Troy.

"Why should I?" said Philoctetes sulkily. "You all left me here to die. Why should I come and save you now?" Odysseus took a deep breath. Philoctetes' wound was really *very* smelly.

"Because Apollo himself has sent a great healer to us, who can cure you (*Please, great Apollo, send one! he prayed silently*), and when that leg is better the gods themselves say you're going to be the one who punishes the man who began all this (*I hope!*). Just think how famous you'll be when you kill that traitor, Paris!"

Finally Odysseus managed to persuade Philoctetes to get into his boat, together with Heracles' bow and arrows. When they got there, Machaon the famous healer had just arrived. (*Thank you, Apollo, thought Odysseus.*) In no time at all, Philoctetes was as good as new.

After Hector's death, Paris had been elected leader of the Trojan army, so as soon as he was cured, Philoctetes took his bow and arrows and went to challenge Paris to an archery contest.

"Ho! Traitor!" he called up to the walls. "Come and fight! Or are you going to be a coward and hide behind Helen's skirts?" Now Paris couldn't bear to be thought a coward, so he took his own bow and arrows and strode out of the gate to face Philoctetes. Both armies stood watching as the two heroes prepared.

Thwack, thwack, thwack! Before Paris could even raise his bow, three of Philoctetes' deadly arrows had hit him. Menelaus ran forward to finish him off, but two Trojan soldiers seized their wounded leader and carried him back to Troy.

"Take me to Mount Ida," groaned Paris, remembering what the nymph Oenone had said when he left her. "My beloved Oenone is the only one who can save me now." But Oenone did not love Paris any more after the way he had treated her.

"Let that wretched Helen cure him," she sniffed angrily, turning her back. So Paris died in agony, and as his soul fled down to the Underworld, Helen shook her head as if she had suddenly woken up from a dream.

"What am I doing here?" she wailed. "And where is my true husband, Menelaus?" Aphrodite's love spell had been broken at last, and the war was nearly over.

Next day the steps up to Athene's Temple were crowded with people. Atticus asked Callimachus to hold Melissa while he went up to make his sacrifice.

"For the Goddess," he whispered, handing his jar of wine to a priestess.

"May she give you a tongue of silk, and the voice of a nightingale!" boomed the priestess. Everybody looked at Atticus and pointed.

"How on earth did that woman know I was in the competition?" he asked Callimachus. Callimachus pointed to the carved red entry stick poking out of Atticus's pocket.

"Easy!" he said. "Now how about another story?"

◫ 87 ◫
The Luck of Troy

Now that Paris was dead, the kings met once more to discuss how they were to defeat Troy and rescue Helen.

"We have done everything that Calchas advised," they said. "So why hasn't Troy surrendered?" Just then Odysseus came in with a prisoner. It was the Trojan prophet Helenus, who had been captured on his way from Troy to Mount Ida.

"Tell us how we can defeat your city, old man!" cried the kings. But Helenus would not betray his people.

"All I will say is this," he said. "A magic statue protects us from harm, and while we have it, Troy will never fall!" Then he went on his way.

"It's up to you, Odysseus," said the kings. "You must sneak into Troy somehow and find out where this magic statue is kept. Then you must steal it and bring it back to us."

It was the most difficult thing Odysseus had ever had to do. How was he to get into the city without being found out? Finally, he dressed up as a beggar and got Diomedes to beat him until the blood ran. Then he crawled to the gate of the city.

"Help me! Help me!" he begged. "Save me from the dreadful Greeks, especially that terrible Odysseus who has given me these painful wounds." The Trojan soldiers took him to King Priam at once. The kind old man had his wounds bathed, and gave him a fresh cloak and a hot meal, and after asking him some questions, to which Odysseus replied with clever lies, he set him free.

"You may live with us," said Priam. "We need all the soldiers we can get."

Now Helen had recognised Odysseus at once, and as he left Priam's palace, she ran after him and beckoned him up to her bedroom.

"You've got to save me and take me back to my dear Menelaus," she said. "I must have been under a spell to run off with that spoilt boy Paris!" Then Odysseus asked her where he could find the magic statue.

"It is called the Luck of Troy, and it's in the Temple of Pallas Athene," she said. "If you stay here with me, I will take you there at nightfall." They spent a delightful afternoon together plotting and planning the defeat of Troy, then, as it grew dark, they went out to the temple.

While Helen distracted the old priestess, Odysseus tiptoed behind the temple pillars and seized the statue from the chest behind the altar. Helen had shown him a secret passage under the walls, and soon he had escaped, muddy but triumphant.

"We have the Luck of Troy, Your Majesties," he said, as he strolled into the Greek camp, holding up the precious object. "I think we can defeat them now! Helen and I have worked out a brilliant plan."

The Trojans shivered in their beds as they heard the wild cheers break out from the ships by the shore. But Helen only smiled.

"I shall soon be free!" she whispered eagerly. "Watch out Troy, the Greeks are coming!"

A day later, they were standing together on the slope by the Great Gate of Troy. "This is where the Wooden Horse stood, isn't it?" asked Callimachus.

"Yes," said Atticus. "My old grandfather used to say it was taller than twenty men."

Callimachus's eyes were round with wonder. "Please, Atticus. Please tell me the story. I'll do anything for you . . ."Atticus laughed. It looked as if Callimachus of Cyrene was bringing him luck already!

88
The Wooden Horse

The ramparts of Troy were crowded as everybody tried to see what the Greeks were doing behind their high wall. Such a hammering and banging, such a bustle and hustle hadn't been heard or seen since they had arrived, ten whole years ago.

"They'll attack tomorrow," said the gloomy ones among them, as they heard the sound of axes being sharpened.

But as the next day dawned, bright and sunny, the Trojans had a great surprise when they looked out from the ramparts again. No tents, no horses, no men, no ships, no fires—not a trace of the Greeks was left on the shore. Only the high wall remained, and behind that was something so strange that the Trojans poured out of the gates to look at it. It was a huge wooden horse, the height of twenty men. Its mane was painted royal purple, it had great staring eyes made of red and green stones, and its harness was painted gold on its jet-black body. There was a notice tied around its neck. '*An offering to Athene for our safe return to Greece*' it said in large letters.

The Trojans danced and sang with joy. They were free at last!

"Let us take this beautiful thing into the city, and put it in front of Athene's temple!" they cried. But Priam and his counsellors were not so sure.

"Perhaps it is a trick," they said. "Perhaps an army of heroes is hiding inside!" So they stuck spears into the horse's belly, and wiggled them around. But not a sound was heard. Then Helen stepped forward.

"I have an idea," she said. "If there are Greek heroes hiding in there, they will not be able to resist the sound of their wives' voices—after all they haven't seen them for ten years. When I was born, the gods gave me the gift of imitation. I can imitate all their wives so perfectly that if the heroes are in there, they will come out straight away." Priam and his counsellors thought this was brilliant, so Helen walked round the horse calling each hero by name.

"Oh Odysseus," she called in Penelope's voice. "Oh Menelaus, beloved, it is I, your Helen." Each of the heroes she called in turn, but none replied, as she had arranged with Odysseus.

"There," she said to Priam. "You see, it's perfectly safe." So the Trojans pulled the horse into the city. It was so huge that they had to take the gates off their hinges to get it through, but at last it was pulled to its resting-place in front of Athene's temple. Everybody was so exhausted that they went to bed very early.

"We will dedicate the horse to Athene in the morning," they murmured sleepily. But in the dead of night a trapdoor in the horse's belly opened, and out poured all the heroes of the Greek army. Helen flashed a bright light from her window to call back the Greek ships which had been hiding behind some islands, and soon they were on their way to Troy once more. Then the heroes cut down the sleepy sentries guarding the open gates and the palace— all except for Menelaus who ran to find Helen. The defeat of Troy had begun.

It was the day before the competition started, and everybody was making their way to the amphitheatre on Mount Ida to make sure of a good spot. Several people were clutching carved coloured sticks like Atticus's red one.

"I was wondering . . ." said Callimachus from Melissa's other side.

"Whether I could tell you a story," finished Atticus. "I'm not sure I should. It might look like showing-off with all these other storytellers around."

"Oh, go on," said Callimachus. "No one will hear you except me. And you did promise to tell me about the sack of Troy . . ."

89

The Greeks Go Home

Many dreadful deeds were done in the streets of Troy that night, and few escaped. The Greeks showed little mercy, and soon the sky was lit with flames and smoke, and the cries of the wounded were heard even by the gods on Olympus. Hera and Athene looked at each other and smiled. Their revenge on Paris's birthplace was nearly complete.

Menelaus fought his way through the streets, killing anyone who got in his way. He was desperate to reach his wife. At last he found the house where Odysseus had told him she lived and ran up the stairs. At the door stood one of Hector's brothers, Deiophobus, with his sword drawn.

"You shall not have her," he snarled. But Zeus himself gave strength to Menelaus's arm, and soon Deiophobus lay dead. Menelaus stepped over his body, and went into the room. There was Helen, sitting on the bed, weeping.

He looked at her and remembered all the sorrow she had caused for both Greeks and Trojans alike. But she was still as beautiful as ever, and as she looked up, the tears running down her lovely cheeks like crystal drops of dew, his heart melted, and he dropped his bloody sword and held out his arms.

"It was not your fault, my love," he said quietly. "It was the will of the gods. Will you come home to Greece with me?" And Helen ran to him and kissed him and kissed him as if she would never stop.

As they walked away together towards the Greek ships, hand in hand, the city of Troy went up in fountains of fire. The spires of the palace came crashing down, and the tall gate towers crumbled into a heap of stone. As dawn broke, only a smoking ruin was left. The great city of Troy was no more and the long war was over at last.

"And then did they all just go home?" asked Callimachus as they arrived on the lower slopes of the mountain. Atticus looked round. He could hear the crash of thunder in the distance.

"Looks like a sea-storm's building," he said. "Let's make ourselves and Melissa a proper shelter under this boulder, and then I'll tell you the last story about the Trojan War. After that I shall have to rest my voice. It's my big day tomorrow, and you wouldn't want me to be hoarse!"

90
The Princess Nobody Believed

The Greeks were now free to return to their homes and families after ten long years. They loaded their ships with looted treasures and slaves, and prepared to depart. But as the sails went up, a fierce wind rose, preventing them from leaving the harbour.

"Not again!" groaned Menelaus and Agamemnon, and they sent for Calchas the soothsayer to find out what the problem was.

Now one of the Greek heroes was a man called Ajax. He was a strong, brave man, and a brilliant runner and javelin player. But he also had a terrible temper. When the belly of the wooden horse had opened, he had been one of the first out. He had headed straight for the Temple of Athene, where he knew there would be plenty of treasure.

"And perhaps I shall capture some slaves, too," he thought greedily. Ajax liked owning slaves. It made him feel important. As he entered the temple, he noticed a girl hiding behind a pillar. His first slave! He dragged her out by the hair and tied her up, even though she screamed and clung to the altar and prayed out loud to the goddess.

"Woe!" screamed the girl. "Woe to him who makes the priestess Cassandra a slave. He shall be struck by Zeus himself!" But Ajax took no notice, and anyway he didn't believe that the ruler of the universe was going to bother about one puny slave girl, even if she did claim to be some priestess.

How wrong he was!

Little did Ajax know that Cassandra was the daughter of King Priam. One day she had been picking violets by a stream when Apollo had come by. He had fallen in love with the beautiful princess. But she would have nothing to do with him.

"I am going to be a seer and tell the future," she said. "I don't have time to fall in love with gods." This made Apollo so furious that he put a terrible curse on her.

"You will indeed see the future, Cassandra—in fact you will be my sister Athene's priestess," he said. "But the trouble is that nobody will believe what you say." And it was true— Cassandra predicted all sorts of things, some good, some bad—but no one ever believed a word of it.

Calchas closed his eyes and looked for a sign from the gods. Quite soon he began to speak. He told Menelaus and the other kings how badly Ajax had treated Cassandra.

"He must be punished," he cried loudly. "For the gods themselves have marked her for their own." Ajax was furious. He lost his temper completely and tried to fight everyone who came aboard his ship. But finally Cassandra was saved and taken back to the shore.

"I don't believe in the wretched gods!" cried Ajax, shaking his fist at the sky. The wind dropped for a moment, and he ordered his ship to set sail at once. "I don't need any of you," he yelled in a rage.

It does not do to mock the gods, and as soon as Ajax's ship had left the safety of the harbour, it hit a huge rock. The ship began to sink.

"Come and get me, Zeus!" cried Ajax, laughing madly and dancing on the tilting deck. This was too much. Zeus sent down a thunderbolt while Poseidon aimed his trident and together they sank Ajax and his ship to the bottom of the sea.

Then the winds fell and the waves were calm, and the rest of the Greek fleet sailed away from Troy forever. But not all of them reached home, and some travelled a long and weary road, and had many adventures before they got there. Troy was rebuilt in time, but it was never again as great as it had been under King Priam and his brave sons and daughters.

Early on the first day of the competition, a single trumpet note rang out to call everyone to the amphitheatre. Atticus hurried towards the arena, straightening his best robes and clutching his red stick and the lucky pebble his children had given him before he left Crete. Two hundred and forty-nine other storytellers hurried with him. When the sacrifices to the gods were over, the Thirty-Ninth Mount Ida storytelling festival was declared open.

"We will now draw the stories for each group of competitors," shouted the chief judge. He stuck his hand into a big leather bag and pulled out a red stick. Then he stuck his other hand into a huge brass jar and pulled out a slip of parchment.

"Red Group!" he cried. Atticus and twenty-four others moved forward nervously. "You will each tell a story about Odysseus." The crowd cheered.

Minutes later the Red Group judges had given everyone a numbered disc. Atticus looked down at his. 'One' it said in large letters. He was first. Slowly he walked out in front of the judges and began.

91
The Land of Sleep

Of all the heroes who conquered Troy, Odysseus, King of Ithaca was the most cunning. He was craftier than a fox, cleverer than a snake, and wilier than a wolf in goat's clothing. But even he could not escape the fate that Zeus had planned for him, although he tried very hard.

"Perhaps Zeus has forgotten that he told the oracle I couldn't go home for another ten years," he said to himself. "Maybe if I just sail home very quietly, Zeus won't notice." So he sneaked away from Troy with his twelve ships and set a course for Ithaca.

Almost immediately a great storm blew up, and the ships were blown hither and thither, up and down and round and round, until their sails were in rags and their sailors were drooping with weariness.

"Oh dear!" said Odysseus on the ninth day, when the winds had died down and the ships had come to rest on a strange shore far far away from his beloved home. "Zeus hasn't forgotten me after all." But he was a brave man, and he wasn't going to be put off by a little bad luck.

"This looks like an interesting place," he said to his sailors, and he sent out three of his men to go and explore, while he and the others mended the ships as best they could, or rested in the warm sunshine. Hours went by, and more hours, and soon it was getting dark. The men had not returned.

"I suppose I shall have to go out and look for them," sighed Odysseus.

Now the place where Odysseus and his ships had landed was filled with a strange forgetting magic. The people who lived there were called the Lotus-Eaters. They were all very beautiful and they ate nothing but a sweet juice which they made from the petals of a white flower that grew in the pools and rivers.

They dressed in robes of gold and silver, and they lived high in the treetops, where they sang like birds, and danced in the branches.

Odysseus tramped through the dark forest all night, but just after sunrise he came to a green glade, with a silver cloth spread in the middle of it. His three men were sprawled asleep on the grass, each clutching a golden cup. Above him sounded faint laughter and the twittering of birdsong. He shook the men roughly and their sleepy eyes opened.

"Noo!" they groaned. "Go away, whoever you are! We want more lotus juice!"

"Come on, you three," said Odysseus sternly. "What about your wives and children waiting at home in Ithaca?" But the men just smiled stupidly and asked him where Ithaca was.

"More lotus juice," they cried. "More wonderful, marvellous lotus juice is all we want for the rest of our lives." The treetops shook and shivered with invisible giggles as the Lotus-Eaters looked down on Odysseus and his men.

In the end poor Odysseus had to go back all the long long way through the forest and fetch the rest of the crew to drag them back to the ships. And for days afterwards the three men had to be tied to the mast to stop them jumping into the sea and trying to swim back to the land of the Lotus-Eaters.

"Let's try again," said Odysseus as he gave the order to set sail for Ithaca once more. But Odysseus's adventures weren't over yet—oh no! Zeus had planned many many more exciting things for the years to come, and his return to Ithaca was a long, long way off.

The judge was reading out the list of those who had got through to the second day. Atticus hugged Callimachus when he heard his name called.

"I did it!" he cried.

"Of course you did," snorted Callimachus. "You were the best by far. Now hush! You're supposed to listen."

The judge was talking again. "Those in the two Copper Groups will each tell five stories. One today, and two on each of the following days." When he had finished explaining, he handed each competitor a copper disc.

"What did you get?" asked Callimachus.

"The story about the Cyclops," Atticus whispered. "One of my favourites."

92
The One-Eyed Giant

On the island of Sicily there lived a most terrible giant called Polyphemus, together with his six brothers. He was a son of Poseidon, and he was one of the race of Cyclopes, who only have one huge bright blue eye, set right in the middle of their foreheads.

Now after Odysseus had left the land of the Lotus-Eaters, Zeus had sent another great storm, which had blown him and his ships this way and that and back and forth until they didn't know where they were or what day of the week it was. So when they saw a huge grassy island, covered in the most wonderful fat sheep and goats, they were overjoyed.

"Drop the anchors!" cried Odysseus. "Lower the boats! We will take a few jars of our best wine and buy some of those sheep from whoever owns them.

Then we will all have a big feast." The sailors danced and cheered, because they were all very hungry after so long at sea.

Odysseus and eleven of his best men got into the boats and rowed for the shore. When they had landed, they walked up a steep rocky path, carrying the wine carefully so as not to drop it, until they came to an enormous cave.

"Pick out some nice juicy-looking sheep while we're waiting for the shepherd to come home," ordered Odysseus. "We don't want to waste any time."

Just as the men had driven ten fat sheep into the cave, they heard a roaring and a stamping and the rocks around them began to shake. Terrified, they ran to the back of the cave and hid behind a large stone. In marched a dreadful looking giant. He sat down in the doorway and called out in a harsh voice:

"Come, come my flocks and herds. Come to Polyphemus and be milked." Odysseus gasped. He had heard of Polyphemus and he knew they were in trouble. When Polyphemus had finished, he lit a crackling fire in the cave. As the flames grew bright, he noticed the twelve Ithacans hiding behind the stone.

He gave a great roar of anger. "Strangers!" he growled. "Sheep-stealers! I shall tear you limb from limb, and eat you for my supper!" And the next second he had seized two of Odysseus's men and had stuffed them into his mouth and crunched them up. Then he rolled a heavy boulder in front of the cave entrance and lay down to sleep. As his snores echoed round the cave, Odysseus tried frantically to think of a plan. But it was no good. The next morning the giant seized two more of his men and  crunched them up as before. Then he went out to see to his flocks, rolling the boulder back behind him as he went. Odysseus and his men were trapped!

As he paced up and down in the dim light, trying to think, Odysseus noticed a large log of wood lying on the ground. It gave him an idea.

"Come on, you men," he called. "Come and help me sharpen this to a point."

"We shall all be eaten up!" groaned his men despairingly. But Odysseus chivvied them and bullied them until he had a long sharp pointed stake.

Just as he was hiding it in a corner, Polyphemus came back. As before, he milked his flocks, and then he grabbed two more men and ate them. He burped loudly and lay back after rolling the boulder in front of the door, but this time he didn't go to sleep. At once Odysseus stepped forward.

"Perhaps you would like some wine after your meal, great Cyclops!" he said timidly. The giant reached out his enormous hand.

"Don't mind if I do," he said. "Tell me your name, little shrimp, so that I can drink your health."

"My name is Nobody," said Odysseus cunningly.

"Very well, Nobody," said the giant. "If you give me some more of this wine I shall give you a gift. I shall promise to eat you last of all your men!" And he laughed horribly, and glugged down another jar. Soon he was snoring like a volcano.

"Right, men," said Odysseus. "Let's get out of here." They heated the point of the stake in the fire and then with a great heave they plunged it into Polyphemus' eye and blinded him.

The giant leapt up with a roar and danced around the cave. Sheep, goats and men scattered out of the way of his galumphing feet. He made so much noise that his six brothers came to see what was happening.

"Who is hurting you?" they cried.

"Nobody!" yelled Polyphemus. "Nobody is!" The other giants looked at each other and shrugged.

"He must have a bad belly-ache," they said to each other as they went away. Early the next morning as Polyphemus rolled the boulder away to let out his flocks, Odysseus tied his five remaining men underneath the five largest sheep. Odysseus himself clung underneath the ram, holding his breath as Polyphemus felt along each sheep's back to see if he and his men were escaping. As soon as they were out of the cave they ran back to the boats as fast as they could, taking as many sheep as would fit.

How relieved they all were to sail away from that terrible island. But as they sailed past Polyphemus's cave, Odysseus made a big mistake.

"Ho! Polyphemus!" he shouted. "You have not been tricked by Nobody after all. I am King Odysseus of Ithaca!" Polyphemus heard him, and roared out a curse.

"Let my father, Poseidon, god of the sea, punish you!" he cried. And Poseidon heard him. Now Odysseus had not one, but two powerful gods working against him. Would he ever get home to Ithaca after this?

It was the third day of the Festival and Atticus beamed delightedly. People kept coming up and congratulating him on how well he had told his Cyclops story, and now Captain Nikos and the crew had turned up.

"I hear you're the best of the bunch," roared Nikos.

"Not really," said Atticus. "And there's still a long way to go till the end of the competition."

"We'll be cheering you on," said Nikos, as Atticus walked out to tell his first story of the day.

93

The Enchantress and the Pigs

Aeolus, the Keeper of the Winds, waved goodbye to Odysseus's fleet as it left his island.

"Remember what I told you, Odysseus," he called. "Don't open that little bag I gave you till you are safely home!"

As the soft westerly breeze blew on, Odysseus lay back on the deck with a tired sigh and slept. As the sun rose on the second day the fleet came within sight of Ithaca. The smoke could be seen rising from the chimneys of his palace, and still he slept on.

"What do you think is in that bag?" said the sailors to one another. "Do you think it could be gold? Or jewels? Or a magic gift? Surely it wouldn't hurt to have just one little peek. We're nearly home after all, and Odysseus is asleep, he'll never know." So they crept up to the sleeping man and untied the strings. As they bent over to see what was inside, there was a tremendous whooshing and swooshing noise and they were all blown backwards. Above the ship the three fierce winds which Aeolus had trapped in the little bag fought and battled and whipped up a great storm which blew the ships apart and scattered them all over the oceans.

"What have you done?" cried Odysseus, as he woke with a jump. "Now we shall never get home!" And he buried his head in his hands and wept.

Of the twelve ships battered by that awful storm, only Odysseus's survived. It eventually came to land safely on a little wooded island covered in oaks and beeches and other tall forest trees.

Fierce-looking lions and tigers and wolves prowled on the shore, but instead of roaring and howling, they purred and whined and rolled over to have their bellies tickled. Odysseus sent his friend Eurylochus and twenty-two men to investigate. They followed the capering, leaping beasts into the forest, and soon they came to a higgledy-piggledy house in a clearing, with vines growing round the door. A feast was set out on long tables, and a pretty woman with long golden hair was waiting at its head. It was Circe, the Enchantress of the Isle of Dawn.

"Come and eat!" she said. "All guests are welcome at my table!" The twenty-two sailors rushed forward and started grabbing at the delicious food and stuffing it into their mouths. Eurylochus was suspicious, though, and hid behind a tree. Suddenly he saw Circe whip out a wand from behind her back and tap each sailor on the top of his head. What happened next was horrible. A loud grunting and squealing noise came from each man's mouth, and as they got up from the table, he saw that they had all been turned into hairy pigs.

"Into the sty with you, you greedy things," said Circe. Eurylochus ran straight back to Odysseus to tell him what had happened.

Odysseus seized his sword and dashed off to the rescue. But on his way he met the god Hermes.

"Not so fast, my friend," said Hermes. "You'll need this!" And he gave Odysseus a small white flower with a black root. "If you have this in your pocket she won't be able to enchant you," he said, grinning. "But don't tell Zeus or Poseidon that I helped you!"

Odysseus thanked the god, and soon he had reached Circe's house. As before a delicious feast was set out, and Circe welcomed her guest with kind words. Odysseus ate and drank thankfully—he was very hungry after the storm. But when Circe crept up behind and tapped him with her wand, nothing happened. She stared at the wand and shook it hopefully, muttering some magic words, but still her enchantment didn't work. Then she laughed and went to the sty where she turned all the pigs back into men.

"You have beaten me, great Odysseus," she said. "You and your men must stay with me for a year while you mend your ship, and then I will help you to get home."

Odysseus agreed happily, but you may be sure that he took her wand away and made Circe promise not to do any more of her enchantments while he and his men were on her magic island.

The clapping had stopped and the crowd was buzzing expectantly. Atticus could see Captain Nikos and the crew and Callimachus sitting together in the shade. He looked at the judges. They were smiling and scribbling on their wax tablets. The last storyteller had been very good.

"Atticus of Crete!" called the judges.

Atticus strode confidently into the arena for his second turn. "The tale of Odysseus and Tiresias," he announced.

94
Ghosts From the Underworld

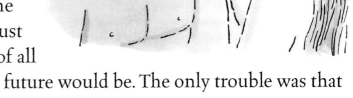

As Odysseus sailed away from the Isle of Dawn, Circe set an enchanted mist around his ship.

"Even Zeus cannot see through this," she said, "and it will protect you as long as no one on your ship sneezes three times in a row." Circe had told Odysseus that before he could go home to Ithaca, he must first go and see Tiresias, greatest of all the Greek seers, to learn what his future would be. The only trouble was that Tiresias was dead and lived down in Tartarus.

"How on earth do I get to Tartarus?" asked Odysseus. "Surely I can't sail to the Underworld?" But Circe nodded.

"If you sail north-west into a northerly wind and follow the stream of Ocean till you come to Persephone's grove of black poplars and willows, you will find the gates of the Underworld on your left-hand side," she said, and then she told him just what to do when he got there.

Now sailing north-west into a northerly breeze is normally quite impossible, but with Circe's magical help Odysseus's ship soon landed on the shore just by Persephone's grove. There he dug a trench, which he filled with a mixture of blood and ewe's milk, and waited with his sword drawn. Soon a whispering and a rustling sound came up from the long dark passage behind the gates, and as they creaked open a grey mass of ghosts poured through.

"Blood and milk," they hissed. "Give us blood and milk to drink!" Odysseus held them off with his sword, until Tiresias finally arrived, and very hard work it was. The ghost of the ancient seer bent his head to drink, and then he looked at Odysseus.

"Great danger and great trouble," he said. "I see the years before you and the years behind. What you have conquered so far is nothing to what you will have to face at home from the greedy men who want your wife and your kingdom. But you will win victory at the end with the help of the goddess Athene!"

"But when?" asked Odysseus. "When shall I get home and what dangers shall I face before I get there?" Tiresias was fading away, but Odysseus heard his answer, like a faint whisper in the still air.

"Long years! Long years before you see Ithaca again. Beware the singers, beware the cliffs, beware the taste of the sun god's island cattle." Odysseus bowed and thanked him with tears in his eyes, and then he let the other ghosts drink. He saw many old friends and loved ones that day—his mother, and his old comrades Achilles and Agamemnon—even the ghost of great Heracles himself came to wish him luck. But in the evening he had to return to his ship.

"Atishoo, atishoo, atishoo!" he sneezed as the grey ghostly fog of Tartarus tickled his nose. Circe's magic mist disappeared at once, and Zeus soon saw that Odysseus's ship was sailing on the ocean again.

"Ho! Brother Poseidon!" he called. "Let's see if we can whip up a real storm this time." And the lightning flashed and the thunder roared as the two gods laughed, and Odysseus and his long-suffering crew were driven out amongst the crashing waves once more.

Atticus patted Melissa. "I'm sorry to leave you alone so much," he said. "But they don't allow donkeys to come and watch, I'm afraid." Melissa butted him in the stomach and snuffled into his hand. She was quite happy. Callimachus cut big bunches of dry grass for her every day, and there was a nice stream nearby.

Then the trumpet sounded its single note loudly for the beginning of the fourth day . . .

"Time to go," said Callimachus. "You've got stories to tell."

95
The Death Singers

"**L**and ahoy!" shouted the sailor at the masthead. Odysseus ran to have a look. What he saw made his heart sink right down into his shabby sandals. It was a little island, far off in the distance. On the island was a group of figures. The sun was glinting off the strings of the golden instruments they carried, and a faint sound of music and singing reached his ears.

Odysseus knew he must not panic. Circe had warned him about this terrible place, and he knew just what to do. He ordered his sailors to stuff wax in their ears, and to get out the oars.

"Now row as hard as you can when I give the signal," he commanded them. "Don't look to right or left, and whatever you do don't unblock your ears or we shall all die."

"But what about you, your Majesty?" asked one of his sailors. "What are you going to do?" Odysseus grinned.

"I'm going to be tied to the mast so tightly that I can't possibly escape," he said. "I'm going to be the only man ever to listen to the voices of the Sirens and live!"

The sailors tied Odysseus to the mast, and then they started to row for their lives. The magical music of the golden harps and the singing came closer and closer, and soon Odysseus was screaming for his men to untie him so that he could swim closer to the wonderful sounds. But they could not hear him. He turned to look at the little island. All around it lay the wrecks of a hundred ships, and on its rocky shores lay the skulls and bones of a thousand sailors, all of whom had listened to the fatal song of the Sirens and died trying to reach them.

The four Sirens themselves sat in a lovely meadow of bright summer flowers. They had the faces of beautiful women, but their bodies were covered in shimmering feathers which glittered and glimmered in the sunlight with all the colours of the rainbow.

"Come to us!" they sang in high sweet voices. "Come to us, Odysseus, bravest of brave heroes! We will tell you the future!" Odysseus shouted and threatened his crew, but it was no good, the ropes around him held fast, and soon the island was far behind them, and the spell of the Sirens' song was broken forever.

Odysseus's men untied him and unplugged their ears. "Now perhaps we shall have a bit of peace," they muttered, as they hoisted the sails once again for home. But unfortunately Zeus had another terrible treat in store for them.

The smoke of hundreds of midday cooking fires drifted into the still air, and the cries of the food-sellers rose above the yatter and chatter of the crowds. More and more people were pouring in to listen to the storytellers, and in corners behind stalls and tents bets were being taken.

"25-1 on Atticus of Crete to get to day five," hissed a quiet voice as Atticus passed. Atticus smiled. He didn't think he had much hope of getting through to the top ten, but you never knew. He turned into the arena and sat down in a shady corner. There was just time for a nap before he was called to perform.

96
Snaptooth and Watersucker

Not many weeks after they had escaped from the Sirens, Odysseus and his men came to an even greater danger, and this time there was no escape.

To get home to Ithaca they had to sail through a narrow rocky passage with high cliffs on either side. On one side of the cliffs, high up in a cave, lived the dreadful monster, Scylla, who had six bright green heads, each on a long snaky neck. Each head had a set of snapping razor teeth, and every time a ship sailed past Scylla would reach down and snatch a sailor in each of her six mouths. Then she would crunch and chew the poor men until their bones cracked and their blood dripped into the sea below.

237

Deep down in the sea at the other side of the passage lived another terrible monster called Charybdis, a fat bubble-like thing, with a huge mouth and blubbery lips. She sat at the bottom of the ocean, sucking and blowing, blowing and sucking, until the water above swirled into spouts and whisked into whirlpools so big that no ship could survive being caught in them.

Circe had warned Odysseus about these monsters too.

"You will have to go through them," she said. "But whatever you do, don't go near Charybdis, who lives on the right. You may lose some men to Scylla, but at least you will survive. If you get caught by Charybdis, you will all die." So Odysseus thought up a crafty plan. He told his men about the danger of the water-sucking monster, but he didn't say anything about the one in the cliff above.

"If I tell them about Scylla," he thought, "they'll be too afraid to go through at all." As the helmsman steered carefully past the dreadful Charybdis, there was a whistling sound. Six sailors were snatched into mid air, and as their horrified companions watched, they were gobbled up in a minute.

"Row! Row for your lives!" roared Odysseus, seizing an oar. And row they did. Soon they had landed far away on a lovely green island where shining black and white and red cattle grazed among the long juicy grass.

"A feast!" cried the men. "Let us have a feast!" But Odysseus remembered Tiresias's warning, and ordered them not to touch the cows.

"We still have some of the provisions Circe gave us," he said. "Let us eat those instead. We shall offend the sun god himself if we eat these cattle, and Zeus knows we can't afford to do that!" But soon another storm rose up, preventing them from leaving the island, and after weeks and weeks of rain and wind all the food was gone. The men got so hungry that Odysseus could not stop them killing and cooking one small cow, although he

himself refused to touch a bite. As soon as the last mouthful had been eaten, the storm dropped and the sun came out. Odysseus and his men hurried to their ship and cast off.

"See!" said the sailors. "It didn't do any harm." Just at that moment Helios the sun god noticed that one of his precious cows was missing. He gave a great roar of anger, and the storm came back stronger than ever. Helios was so angry that he got Zeus to throw a thunderbolt at the ship, which split it in half. All the sailors drowned except Odysseus, who clung on to the mast and keel, which he tied together to make a raft.

By the morning he was being blown back towards Scylla and Charybdis, and even crafty Odysseus was in despair. But just above the whirlpool grew a little fig tree, and as Charybdis sucked down the mast and keel, Odysseus made a great leap and clung to it until the bits of wood appeared again. He dropped down on them and floated away to safety. His bravery and spirit were so great that Zeus finally took pity on him and hid him from the monsters' eyes. Exhausted, he lay there and let the winds and waves blow him where they wanted. For nine days and nine nights he rocked and drifted on the cradle of the ocean. And on the tenth day he was washed through a magical mist and onto the shores of the Island of Ogygia, which, although he didn't know it then, was where he would spend the next seven years of his life.

Nine names had been read out so far, and Atticus was not among them. The judge cleared his throat.

"And the last successful competitor is . . . Atticus of Crete." There was a storm of clapping and cheering. Atticus felt quite faint and had to be held up by Callimachus and Captain Nikos. He had got through to the fifth day!

The judge shook Atticus by the hand. "Well done!" he said. "Now you have to choose the two stories you will tell today".

"Odysseus has brought me luck so far," said Atticus. "I'll tell the stories of Calypso and Nausicaa."

"A good choice," said the judge.

97
The Island of Mists

Odysseus stared out through the magical mist that prevented him leaving the Island of Ogygia, tears running down his cheeks as they had done every day for the last seven years. Although the beautiful nymph, Calypso, who ruled the island, had given him his every desire, Odysseus was unhappy. What use were jewelled swords, and baths of asses' milk, and armour as light as silk and endless endless parties when all he wanted was to go home to his wife Penelope and his son, Telemachus.

"He must be a man by now," wept Odysseus. "And I haven't been there to teach him any of the things a father should. Someone else will have taught him to use a sword, and to ride a horse, and to plough a field.

Someone else will have taught him to sail a ship and to throw a spear." Then he prayed to the goddess Athene to help him. Athene was very fond of Odysseus, but she had not dared to go against her father Zeus and her uncle Poseidon. However, Poseidon was away from Olympus and Athene begged Zeus to allow the wandering hero to return home at last.

"Please, father," she said, fluttering her long silver eyelashes. "You know how you admire his bravery." So Zeus commanded Hermes to fly down to Calypso and order her to let Odysseus go.

Calypso cried and cried, because she really did love Odysseus, but she had to obey Zeus.

"I shall even help him to build a raft," she sniffed as she went to find Odysseus and tell him the good news.

Odysseus whistled and sang as he chopped down trees for the raft. Calypso and her maidens sat sadly beside him as they wove strong ropes to lash it together. Finally it was ready. Calypso loaded it with provisions and gave Odysseus many presents, including a wonderful embroidered robe she had made herself.

The silken sail was raised, and the raft moved slowly out to sea.

"Remember me," cried Calypso as she waved goodbye to the man she loved. And Odysseus raised his hand in farewell as the curtains of mist opened in front of him and he sailed out onto the ocean once more.

"Bad luck," said the competitor who had just sat down next to Atticus.

"What?" said Atticus, waking up with a start. "What do you mean?"

"The lists have just gone up for this afternoon," said the man, laughing unpleasantly. "And you're going right at the end. The judges will be bored by then."

"My old mother always told me that the best comes last," said Atticus. The man grunted and spat as he moved away.

"He's just jealous that I chose such good stories," Atticus said to Callimachus. But as the long hot afternoon drew on and the judges drooped and snored, he wasn't so sure.

98
The Golden Ball

Poseidon waved away Iris the messenger as he peered at the magic map of his ocean kingdom which lay spread out before him.

"I'm busy," he said, frowning fiercely as she tried to hand him Zeus's letter telling him that Odysseus was now free to go home.

While he watched, he noticed a small speck setting off from Calypso's island. As it  grew bigger, he saw that it was a man on a raft—a man he knew and hated.

"Wretched Odysseus!" he roared, and he swirled his trident so hard that the waves rose up as high as houses. The raft was flung into the air, and all the precious gifts that Calypso had given Odysseus sank to the bottom of the sea. Odysseus himself was thrown into the cold rough water.

His embroidered robes became so heavy and soggy that they started to drag him down as he struggled to stay afloat.

"Athene!" he gurgled as he fought to get out of his clothes. "Help me!" As he spoke, a seagull flew over and dropped a silken veil on the water.

"Tie that around you," she screeched. "It will save you from drowning!"

Odysseus tied the veil around his waist and began to swim. He swam and swam and swam until he was exhausted. But the magical veil held him up above the waves and at last he floated to the shores of another island. He crawled into a grove of trees by a little stream, pulled some dry leaves over him, and fell into a deep sleep.

He was woken by giggles and peals of laughter. Sitting up, he saw a group of girls playing with a golden ball, while others washed clothes in the stream. Suddenly the ball bounced and came to rest just by his feet. The tallest girl ran after it and when she saw Odysseus she let out a little scream.

"Don't be afraid," said Odysseus. "I am Odysseus of Ithaca. If you will take me to the king of this place, I will explain everything." The girl, whose name was Nausicaa, happened to be King Alcinous's daughter. She gave Odysseus some clothes, and took him up to the palace, where her father was delighted to receive such a famous hero.

"Welcome to Phaecia! We all thought you were dead long ago," he said, and after giving Odysseus a magnificent feast, King Alcinous gave him many rich gifts to replace those he had lost, as well as a crew and a boat to take him back to Ithaca.

Odysseus fell asleep on the voyage home, and so the king's sailors carried him gently off the boat and laid him down on the shores of his own land at long last, stacking his gifts at his feet.

Now Poseidon was so angry with King Alcinous for helping Odysseus that he turned the king's ship and all its sailors to stone on their voyage home to Phaecia. King Alcinous had to sacrifice twelve of his best bulls to Poseidon to stop him dropping a great stone mountain on the harbour.

"That's the very last time I help some handsome hero you've picked up off the beach," he said crossly to Nausicaa. But Nausicaa just smiled.

The last five had just been announced. Atticus had got through! The crowd surged around him and his four fellow storytellers, patting backs and shouting, while the judges waved their hands and called for quiet. Finally, one of them seized a great brass gong and beat it till silence fell. He held out a leather bag filled with silver discs.

"Atticus of Crete will pick a story first," he said.

Atticus stepped forward and stuck his hand into the bag. The discs felt cold—all except one. "This one," he said, pulling it out and looking at it. "The Return of Odysseus," he read out loud.

99
The Return of the Wanderer

When Odysseus woke up, he didn't know where he was at all.

"What is this place?" he asked sleepily as he stretched and yawned.

There was a handsome shepherd boy leaning against a nearby tree. The shepherd boy laughed, and as he did so he changed into a tall, beautiful woman wearing silver armour and a winged helmet.

"Don't you recognise your own kingdom?" said Athene. "Shame on you, Odysseus!" Odysseus looked around him and soon he saw that the goddess was right. He was home at last! He knelt down and kissed the ground as he wept with relief.

"No time for that," said Athene sternly. "Now that you are here, there is a lot of work to do. All the young men around are trying to marry your wife because they think you are dead, and your poor son is trying to protect her as well as your wine and food, which they are drinking and eating by the bucketful." Odysseus looked around wildly for his sword, but Athene stopped him.

"You will just get yourself killed if you do that," she said, shaking him. "I have a better plan." After she had helped Odysseus to hide the treasure and gifts which King Alcinous had given him, she disguised him as an old beggar man and sent him off to find his old swineherd, Eumaeus, warning him to tell no one who he really was.

"Wait for me at Eumaeus's hut, and I shall bring someone you will want to meet," she said with a little smile.

Eumaeus was a kind old man, and when he saw the wretched beggar at his gates he asked him in and gave him food and wine from his own meagre store.

"Perhaps the gods will look more kindly on me if I share what I have with a stranger," he said sadly. "I don't think things can get much worse than they already are around here." As Odysseus huddled unnoticed in a corner, munching some cheese, a young man strode in.

"Master Telemachus," cried Eumaeus with a shout of joy. Odysseus looked at the son he had not seen for twenty years, and his eyes filled with tears of pride. Telemachus was tall and strong and handsome—everything a prince of Ithaca should be. Eumaeus went out to shut up his pigs for the night, and as soon as he had left a shining mist appeared in the room and Athene stepped out. She took a surprised Telemachus by the hand and led him over to the dark corner, where Odysseus was sitting quietly. As she lifted the beggar's disguise, Telemachus saw a tall man standing before him. The man was built like a hero, and he was smiling.

"Father?" said Telemachus in a whisper.

"My son!" said Odysseus, holding out his arms. After much hugging and weeping, Athene led them both out of the hut.

"We must keep your father's return a secret," she said to Telemachus. "No one must know, not even Eumaeus or your mother. I shall disguise your father as a beggar again and take him to the palace. There he can see what kind of men are courting Penelope, and we shall make a plan to get rid of them."

As the beggar Odysseus entered his courtyard an old hound lifted his head and wagged his tail. Odysseus brushed away a tear as he recognised his best hunting dog, Argus. "At least my dog greets me properly," he muttered sadly to himself. "This is not the homecoming I had planned at all."

Odysseus soon saw the sort of greedy, rude and unpleasant men who were infesting his palace like rats. Although it was the custom to treat beggars kindly, they kicked him and threw him out onto the dungheap, jeering and laughing at his rags.

"Find yourself another spot, old greybeard," they shouted as they returned to feasting on the best of Odysseus's wine and foods.

"Just you wait," growled Odysseus, rubbing his bruised shoulder. "Just you wait."

The crowd strained forward to listen. It was so quiet in the great arena that even the judge's small cough sounded like one of Zeus's thunderclaps.

"The three Golden Storytellers of the Thirty-Ninth Mount Ida storytelling festival are as follows." The silence grew even deeper.

"Timon of Byzantium." The crowd cheered as a dark, curly-haired man with a wide grin stepped forward waving.

"Corinna of Eleusis." The cheers grew even more wild as a tiny woman with wrinkled apple cheeks hobbled into the arena, blowing kisses to the crowd. Atticus dug his nails into his damp palms. It was now or never.

"Atticus of Crete." The crowd erupted. Atticus found himself being carried shoulder high towards the arena through the shouting, laughing throng. He raised his fists in triumph. He was actually in the final of the greatest storytelling competition in the world, and what's more he knew exactly which story he was going to tell.

100
The End of the Journey

Penelope sat in her bedchamber staring at the wonderful tapestry she had made. For many long years she had held her suitors off by promising that she would marry one of them when it was finished. Each day she had stitched and stitched, but each night she had unpicked most of what she had done to buy just a little more time. Now her trick had been discovered and tomorrow she would have to choose one of the suitors, and the day after that she would have to marry him.

"Oh Odysseus, my love," she sighed. "Where are you? Why don't you come home?" And a single tear ran down her lovely cheek and dropped onto her hand, where it shone like a diamond. At that moment there was a knock at the door. It was the old nurse, Eurycleia.

"Beg pardon, my lady," she said. "But there's an old beggar man asking to see you. He says he has news of Odysseus." Penelope jumped up.

"Bring him in at once," she cried. While Eurycleia bustled round making the old man comfortable, Penelope listened to his story.

"Odysseus will soon be back in Ithaca," said the old beggar. Penelope sighed.

"But how am I to hold off the suitors?" she asked. "I have promised them an answer tomorrow." The old beggar scratched his head.

"Do you still have Odysseus's great bow? The one only he could draw?" Penelope nodded. "Then tell the suitors that whoever can draw the bow and shoot it through twelve axe-rings shall be your next husband." Just then Eurycleia gave a gasp. As she was washing the beggar's feet she noticed a great white scar on his ankle. Only one person had a scar like that!

"Odyss . . ." she started, but Athene clapped an invisible hand over her mouth so she couldn't speak. Odysseus shook his head at her and put his finger to his lips.

The next day, before the usual feast began, Telemachus escorted Penelope down to the hall to speak to the suitors. She held up the great bow and told them what she wanted them to do. Meanwhile Eumaeus bustled about, setting up the axe-heads in a straight row. Each suitor in turn took up the great bow and wrestled with it. Some managed to string it, some even managed to fit an arrow on the string, but none could pull it.

"Is there not one man in this hall who is as good as my husband, Odysseus?" cried Penelope scornfully. Then the old beggar who had been sitting in the corner stepped forward.

"I will try," he said. All the suitors laughed and jeered, and several of them even stepped forward to throw him out again. But Penelope held up her hand.

"Let him try!" she ordered. The beggar stripped off his ragged cloak and the suitors all gasped suddenly at the size of his muscles. He picked up the bow and stroked it. Then he strung it, fixed an arrow to the string and pulled it back to his ear in one swift smooth motion. The arrow whistled as it left the bow and swooshed through every one of the axe-rings. Suddenly a golden mist surrounded the beggar man, and his disguise fell away.

"I am Odysseus!" he cried to the astonished suitors. "And you are no longer welcome in my hall!" The suitors rushed to the walls to pull down the spears that had been hanging there, but Telemachus had taken them away the day before. As Eumaeus locked the doors, Telemachus and Odysseus ran towards the suitors and started killing them, while a terrified Penelope ran to her room and locked herself in.

It was a long and bloody battle, but at last all the suitors lay dead on the floor.

Athene took all the bodies away with a magical sweep of her hand, and soon the hall was clean and sparkling once more. Penelope's door opened a crack and she peeped out into the silence. What she saw made her heart sing with joy. There were her beloved husband and son waiting for her below. A shaft of sunlight turned their robes to pure gold as she flew down the stairs with her arms held wide open.

"Welcome home, my love," she cried softly. "Welcome home at last."

Atticus Comes Home

The judges were taking a long time to decide who had come first. A fat black and gold vase, beautifully painted, stood on the table in front of them. At last the herald stepped forward to blow a fanfare on his trumpet, and a hush fell.

"We have a winner!" boomed the chief judge. "The gods have chosen . . ." he paused dramatically. "Atticus of Crete!"

Captain Nikos and Callimachus and the crowd wept and howled and cheered and

danced, while far away on the edge of the camp a small grey donkey brayed with joy as her master was crowned with the golden laurels of the greatest storyteller in the world.

Atticus and Melissa stopped on the dusty track and looked down at the village. It lay in the late summer sunlight, the little white buildings shining like pearls. Atticus sighed. The journey home had seemed very quick. After they had put Callimachus on the boat back to Cyrene, Captain Nikos had insisted on taking them all the way to Crete, and the winds had been mild and fair all the way into the harbour at Miletus.

"Do you think they're expecting us so soon?" Atticus said to Melissa. Melissa looked at him through her long eyelashes and then she began to trot. Faster and faster she went with Atticus running beside her. There was the shrine to Athene, there was the oil-seller's house, and there was . . . home! A row of figures was standing in the golden sunshine, looking at a cow, a pig, a cockerel and several hens. Atticus stopped in the gateway and held his arms wide, wide, wider, and the figures began to run towards him, shrieking and crying with joy.

"I'm back," he said as he disappeared in a sea of kisses and hugs and a clamour of questions. "I'm back, and I've got something to show you." Atticus went towards Melissa's saddlebags and took out two things. One was a wreath of golden laurels, and the other was a fat black and gold vase full of golden coins. He held them out to his clamouring family, who had fallen silent at last.

"Look!" said Atticus the Storyteller. "I won!"